I0570418

UNMASKED

GENELLA DeGREY

Unmasked
ISBN # 978-1-78430-581-9
©Copyright Genella DeGrey 2015
Cover Art by Posh Gosh ©Copyright April 2015
Interior text design by Claire Siemaszkiewicz
Totally Bound Publishing

Published in 2015 by Totally Bound Publishing, Newland House, The Point, Weaver Road, Lincoln, LN6 3QN, United Kingdom.

Totally Bound Publishing is a subsidiary of Totally Entwined Group Limited.

UNMASKED

Dedication

Ah, Venice. We celebrate your beauty and
uniqueness —

I would like to dedicate this book to all Venetians, past
and present, who have worked to preserve the beauty
and history of the celebrated city of Venice, Italy.
Molti ringraziamenti, miei fratelli e mie sorelle!

And to those of you who adore 'happily ever afters',
here is a double dose.

One more note, and call it artistic license if you will,
but we've slanted the story's historical phrasing
toward a more modern speak for today's readers.
Enjoy!

Chapter One

Venice, Italy, 1795

They call it 'carnal knowledge'. The tension melted from Weston's shoulders. It was nothing short of divine the way certain women just knew how to fulfill a man's desires, such as the one now sucking his cock. Somehow, she'd known every sweet spot, every pressure point on his torso and below that triggered the ultimate bliss in which he was now entrenched. It had taken little effort to lay down his money and body without so much as a few words.

"I wish a room with a bath and a proficient female companion, please," he'd respectfully requested in Italian and slipped a purse-full of silver ducato into the madam's palm. It was likely an overly generous sum, but he was on holiday. And wasn't the whole purpose of saving a hefty portion of one's income all winter long to indulge one's self in pleasures untold in lands far away?

He'd garnered the directions to this recommended establishment from a couple of his well-traveled peers back in London. And oh, how right they'd been to suggest this particular house.

The woman between his legs fondled his balls as her jaw went slack. She grazed the head of his penis against the roof of her mouth and down her throat.

His orgasm was building, but he was in no hurry. He *needed* this. He'd gone without for the longest time since he'd discovered the magic of being buried hilt-deep between a woman's lips — either the top or the bottom set. Either way, didn't matter to him just as long as she was accomplished in the baser arts. So he'd allow her free rein of his body for now. He drew a deep breath and exhaled a moan, sinking further into relaxation.

His sister and her entourage would arrive within mere hours, and he'd be obliged to spend at least one meal per day with them. While he loved his twin sister, he'd much rather spend his time in the luxurious brothels of Venice. Discretion was not foremost in his mind here as it was back at home. No one knew of him in this beautiful city, which would equate to no wagging tongues — save the one licking a circle around his anus at this very moment.

And with a companion who knew the lay of his land, why would he want to be anywhere else?

The woman stopped for a moment to enquire of him in Italian, "Can I do it differently for you?" In her eyes hung what could only be self-doubt.

"No, no. You are doing just fine, love. I'm taking my time not because of your skills — which are exquisite — but for reasons that have to do with my travels. I came directly to this room off the boat from England, you see, and it was an uncomfortable if not awkward crossing, to say the least. So, please continue."

"*Si*," she replied with a grateful grin and licked the head of his cock, drawing it into her mouth once again.

* * * *

Smelling of French-milled soap, Weston waited at the end of the jetty, waving back at his sister as she stood upon the bow of the approaching Royal Navy ship. Slow was the going, but now that he'd been properly gratified by that achingly competent Venetian woman, he'd found a heavenly new patience.

"Weston!" She waved. "You look like you belong here," she shouted above the din of the sailors, scuttling hither and yon.

He smiled at her observation. Had he no other obligations for the rest of his life, he'd surely consider living here. But as it was…

He strode over to the gangplank and, once Gwen reached the bottom, he greeted his twin sister with a tight hug. "Is the Admiral's daughter properly wed, then?"

"Quite. The ceremony at sea was rather impressive. She is now on her honeymoon to her new husband's familial holdings in Austria. We are the last civilians to disembark after the wedding. Admiral Forbes was so accommodating. He lent us his cabin once all the other passengers had gone."

She seemed overly chatty at the moment—even for Gwen—but he ignored the girlish inclination. "And where is Miss Ellie?" His gaze landed at the top of the gangplank. Wherever his sister ventured, her best friend wasn't far behind. He quickly scanned the fore and aft of the portside deck but she was nowhere to be found.

A few sailors swept passed them. "Gwen, where is Ellie?"

Gwen made an unnecessary study of her gloved fingers.

The men who'd just disembarked laughed, drawing Weston's attention. There, just ahead of them, he spotted a young woman, scurrying toward the palazzo of *Signore* Bernardo, the host for their holiday, a leather valise in each hand. He took in the sight of the unmistakable bounce of her lush, chocolate brown curls from below her bonnet and the tiny waist set atop her fashionable, blue silk brocade-draped panniers. It was, without a doubt, Ellie Appleton.

He released his sister. "Gwen?" He'd be the first to admit that his tone was accusatory, but Gwendolyn Rawleigh wasn't exactly the type of girl whom anyone with a brain trusted implicitly.

"Well…"

He waited for her explanation, but when he realized that none was forthcoming, he began to feel the familiar tension creep up his neck.

"Sister, dear, would you be so kind as to enlighten me with the truth?"

Her gaze flickered to Ellie's retreating form and back. "Ellie went to enquire with *Signore* Bernardo about the rooms. Wasn't it kind of him, being an old friend of Father's, to have offered us a stay at his palazzo?"

Ah. She's chatty because she's done something. Good God, what now? "Don't lie to me, Gwen. Ellie wouldn't have gone ten steps without a chaperone." His gaze once again scanned the immediate area. "By the way, where is said faithful dog?" Weston had expected one, if not two elderly companions to disembark from the ship at any moment.

Apparently, Gwen's gloves required yet another inspection.

"You didn't."

At that moment, Gwen's and Ellie's trunks were brought down the gangplank.

"Oh, good. Please take them to Castello 4196, on the Riva degli Schiavoni, and ask for *Signore* Bernardo." She pointed in the general direction of where Ellie had, in her haste, disappeared to. "Come along, Weston."

She made to step around him but he wouldn't permit it. "I want answers, Gwen."

With an irritated huff, she stomped her foot. "Look, I didn't want Ellie's old Aunt Arabella tagging along on my first trip abroad."

"What about your maid, Dashy?"

"I told Dashy and Mama that Aunt Arabella was going to accompany us."

My God. "And you told Ellie's mama and Aunt Arabella that Dashy would be the designated companion."

"Something to that effect."

Whatever tension that Venetian woman had sucked from him was back—with a vengeance. "Are you mad?"

"Shh, Weston. Keep your voice down."

"Don't shush me, Gwen! Have you any idea the level of decorum you've tossed out of the window like a pail-full of rubbish?"

"You've never so much as uttered a peep before—"

"That's because your antics have never tempted fate so that your reputation might be ruined beyond repair!"

"Oh, pish-tosh. There will be nothing to repair, here."

"But society—"

"I don't give a fig about society, the marriage mart or any of it. And besides, who's to know?"

"What of Mama's feelings? I think she'll lock you in your room until your twenty-ninth year when she finds out what you've done."

"She won't find out."

"Yes she will."

"Truly? How?"

Wes opened his mouth but closed it just as quickly. He was well aware that Gwen already knew that he was the type of brother whose adoration went above and beyond to let her get away with anything. It always had been thus, and probably ever would be, much to his chagrin.

Perhaps that's why she felt she could pull this charade off—perhaps he'd spoiled her far too much her entire life.

Yes, it was his fault, for the most part.

"You see? If you don't bring it up, *ever*, no one will be the wiser."

She had him there. "And who will assist you and Ellie with dressing and other necessities?"

"*Signore* Bernardo will have plenty of servants to help, I'm sure."

Damnation. He should demand that they return to London immediately, but he knew he'd have to do nothing short of plucking Gwen from the ground on which she stood and hauling her up the gangplank, which would never do. He knew no one here in Venice who might be able to stand in as escort to his sister and Ellie, save the proprietor and a couple of the women of the *Palazzo d'Amore* he'd just come from. "Well, who —?"

"The answer to the inquiry now dangling from your lips is *you*."

"Me?"

"Of course. When you think about it — who else could do the job of chaperone so well as my own brother?"

It was his turn to stomp his foot. "Gwen, this sort of thing isn't done!"

"And again I say, pish-tosh. There is a first time for every situation. Really, Weston. It's as if you had your own holiday plans in mind."

He sighed and scraped his palm over his mouth and chin. Conceding was the only solution. He couldn't exactly tell his sister that he'd planned on spending his entire trip naked and at the mercy of courtesans.

"There. You see? Now, we have but a few hours before the ball." She succeeded in maneuvering around him this time. "And I don't want you upsetting Ellie, either," she warned over her shoulder at him.

He fell into step by his sister's side. "Of course not. I'm sure she's scared enough as it is."

"For your information, Ellie was only discomfited during the first day at sea."

"Is that why she practically ran for cover a moment ago?"

She fully ignored his inquiry. "The only thing she fears now is your wrath."

"Wrath? When have I ever displayed a single measure of wrath around her — or you, for that matter?"

She peered up at him with the devil's own grin on her face. "Precisely."

Wes clamped his jaw shut. Under the thumb of his twin was not at all where he wanted to be. *Being the responsible one is about to take all the fun out of life.* He shook his head and buried his frustrations as he accompanied his darling twin horror to *Signore* Bernardo's palazzo.

Chapter Two

The moon had risen, full and swollen on the horizon, her face shining with the promise of an eventful evening of delightful excesses.

Gwendolyn Rawleigh sighed. "What could be more decedent than a holiday spent in Venice during *Carnevale*?"

The three happy tourists, Gwendolyn mused, as the trio drifted along the Canale di San Marco in a gondola toward their destination.

A low, thoroughly feminine laugh pulled Gwendolyn's gaze from the moon across the Laguna Veneta, to the arch of a stone bridge that straddled a small waterway less than ten feet away. A scandalized breath caught in her throat as she watched a man raise the hem of the laughing woman's skirt to expose her entire leg from ankle to thigh. It seemed as if she had no underpinnings on at all! Her heart pounded. She couldn't turn her head to look away, even for the sake of decorum — the fact being, she was mesmerized.

The man stroked his hand down the front of his female companion's leg. Gwendolyn could swear she felt the warm caress kiss her own thigh. He dropped to his knees, and just as he did so, the couple went out of view.

She expelled the breath she'd been holding. What had that man been about down on his knees like that? She would certainly like to know. With her cheeks suffused with heat, she focused once again on the watery path ahead of them.

Ellie giggled and turned from the moonrise to Gwendolyn, the bounce of her dark brunette curls echoing her enthusiasm. "Wasn't *Signore* Bernardo vastly agreeable? What a sweet man to have put his entire household at our disposal."

"Mm." Gwendolyn agreed, her thoughts yet astray.

"And I'm so pleased to be here with you and Weston, Gwennie. You both look simply stunning."

Gwendolyn shook off the sensual murmurings in her mind. "Thank you, dear, so do you. I'm certainly happy we're not in London."

Wes grimaced at his sister's comment then turned to Ellie. "I can't wait to hear how you got your mama to allow you to miss the pre-season affairs in order to traipse about the most romantic city in the world with my spinster sister."

"Oh stop, Weston." Gwendolyn gave him a playful slap on the arm, gaining his full attention. "I'm not such a spinster." When standing, her brother's sandy-blond head towered over her by a foot, but her advantage was that she'd been born first.

Weston smirked at her. "Of course you aren't. That's why you've designed to avoid your season in lieu of a trip to the continent."

He spoke the truth, and Gwendolyn knew it. She stamped down a small pang of guilt, refusing to allow it to affect her blissful mood. She was chiefly here to evade the practically unavoidable marriage market she'd been subjected to back in London. Even though her fortune did not dictate the need for a husband, society had its standards, regardless of how ridiculous. And at so many seasons out, she wished to take a chance at making her own choices. Besides, a marriage should be a mutual thing, not some silly prize awarded for the best sow at the fair. "Now, you, hush, or I will pull rank and send you home," she taunted.

"A minute and a half doth not a rank create." Weston said wryly, his gaze delving playfully into her eyes.

"I beg to differ, sir. I could have hitched your cord to Mama's tailbone so that you could not have emerged at all," Gwendolyn shot back, unable to hide her grin.

Ellie gasped at Gwendolyn's words, her blue eyes gone wide.

"Ha! You wish it were so! The only reason you were born first is because I was being polite." He huffed out a lively but exasperated breath at this oft recurring conversation and placed a hand atop her gloved one. He then lowered his voice so that only she could hear. "I know the traditions of our set make your blood boil, Gwen, but remember, Ellie is young and innocent, and may not be as offended as you are."

"I, too, am innocent." The soft undertones of her statement smacked of despondence, but she didn't care.

"Yes, you are. And if I don't keep you so during this trip, mama will have my head — but only after she skins me alive when she finds out *I* took over as chaperone, that is."

Following his tirade he directed his focus on her and in his eyes shone his affinity for her, as it always did following a reprimand. His sympathetic smile warmed her heart. Not only did they have that connection that only twins have, or so she was told, but Weston had her best interests in mind. He'd never forced things on her like Mama did, and she loved him dearly for it.

"Which she won't, but we've already been over that."

He cleared his throat. "In the meantime, let us forget our transgressions and enjoy *Carnevale*."

"That's why *carnevale* was invented, after all."

Gwendolyn turned to gawk at Ellie and noticed that Weston had done the same. "How on earth do you know that?"

Ellie shrugged a dainty shoulder. "I read up on it. This celebration has been going on for hundreds of years! It's all so exciting, don't you agree?"

* * * *

They arrived at the private *palazzo* for their very first ball abroad, and Weston handed each of the girls from the gondola. "Miss Ellie, I trust you won't allow my sister to corrupt you on this trip."

Ellie stepped onto the jetty and gave Weston a crooked smile. "You know better than that, Weston. And shame on you. You sound just like my mama."

Pulling a face, Gwendolyn watched Weston give Ellie's dainty hand a squeeze then winked at her friend.

"Weston, if you coddle Ellie in excess, she'll end up too sheltered and not have a good time."

"Well, what are chaperones for?" he murmured and made sure Gwendolyn had her footing.

They took the stone steps that sat at the threshold of the oaken and iron-bound double doors of the *palazzo*. "These houses are strange, and so close to the water," Ellie commented, tying on her mask.

"Not strange for the inhabitants, I assure you," Weston replied, adjusting his papier mâché visage.

"Ellie just thinks it's strange because it's different," Gwendolyn announced, handing a doorman their invitation.

She and Ellie had been best friends well before her first season out, four years ago. Gwendolyn adored Ellie as if she were the little sister she'd never had, and she was sure that Ellie shared the same feelings of kinship. She almost felt it her duty to guide Ellie in matters of the heart and protect her from the ridiculous tradition and pressure on young ladies that society insisted upon before, during and after 'the season'. She'd seen the way the affluent Appleton family had meticulously guarded their only daughter at every turn, and Gwendolyn thanked God that her mother hadn't done things the same way — especially after her father had passed on.

Even though Ellie had never expressed it, Gwendolyn knew that Ellie appreciated her help. She observed how Ellie listened with rapt attention to the little things Gwendolyn would teach her that every girl should know. Yes, Ellie was quite lucky she had Gwendolyn to instruct her.

Once inside the *palazzo*, the small party ascended a wide marble staircase that spilled out onto a runner of thick red carpeting, then down a long elegant hallway to a splendid dining room. The lavish sight sent tingles up Gwendolyn's back. Moments before she donned her mask, she gazed at the other guests in wonder. She'd always found fancy dress gowns fascinating, but the masks, a required complementary piece to one's costume during *Carnevale*, tipped the scales. Every kind of man, woman and beast—both mythical and non—was represented on the faces of the partygoers. Some masks were adorned with lace and jewels, some were elaborately painted and some were merely black or white. She smiled, wishing she had an assortment of masks from which to choose and attire herself with any time of the year.

"Ellie," Gwendolyn whispered. "I've found my passion."

Ellie's intake of breath mirrored her shock and she turned to Gwendolyn. "How you tend to stir up scandalous feelings, Gwennie."

Smiling at her friend's reaction, Gwendolyn clarified her statement, "The *Carnevale* masks, my dear."

"The masks?"

"You see"—she glanced back at Weston to make sure he was far enough away not to hear—"behind each one lays the promise of a clandestine passionate encounter that will leave you breathless."

"What was that, Gwen?" Weston poked his head between the two girls.

"Needless to say, I was pointing out the décor, Weston. Look at all the candles, El."

"Indeed. It's practically daylight in here!" Ellie readily agreed, as if she could read the train of Gwendolyn's thoughts.

Gwendolyn smiled. She and Ellie's harmonious rapport had come in handy a time or two in their lives. To be honest, her comment to Weston wasn't a lie. Gwendolyn truly was in awe of the room.

The crystal chandlers shimmered and reflected the flames. Light sparkled and danced around the room as if tiny pixies skipped about. The huge mirrors that ran the length of the expanse multiplied the opulent effect, as did the gold leaf molding and buttress combination that crisscrossed the ceiling, separating painted scenes of angels and other celestial beings. Between the dining furniture, the polished marble floor fairly glowed and all the light reflected back to the shining crystal above.

"Look at all the wine." Gwendolyn grinned, her gaze now fixed on the tables. "There are at least four bottles per each party of six."

At the nearest table, Weston pulled out two chairs for his sister and Ellie. "I don't know about you two, but I'm famished." He set his mask above her plate and made to take the seat to the right of Ellie's when Weston glanced toward the entrance. "Albert," Weston shouted above the din of the room and waved his hand. "Over here."

Out of decorum, Weston presented his friend. "Girls, you know Albert Pedley, of course?"

Gwendolyn turned to her brother. "What is *he* doing here?" she whispered while Albert bowed and made pleasantries with Ellie.

Weston shrugged a shoulder. "I invited him. Wasn't all that sure he'd show, to be honest."

She blew out an exasperated breath. She'd always thought that Albert seemed like a sneaky weasel, with his dull brown, deeply widow-peaked hair and muddy hazel eyes that were entirely too close together for her taste. None of his visual impediments would have been a problem if his personality hadn't matched his looks so well. "Weston, you know I can't abide the man."

"Oh, Gwen, don't be that way."

"I'm sorry, dear brother. Something deep inside won't allow me to trust him."

"Shush now, or the poor chap will hear you."

"Poor chap, indeed," she grumbled, "I dare say he won't have heard anything different from what he's already aware of." She glanced over her shoulder at the offender. "Look at him drooling over poor Ellie. Can't you make him stop?"

Ellie giggled at something Albert said.

Weston cleared his throat. "Albert, my boy, you've arrived just in time for supper."

Albert turned to them and smiled. "Thank you for inviting me to join you. There is nothing like a respite with old friends." Albert nodded a greeting to Gwendolyn and sat next to Ellie.

Gwendolyn put little effort into her greeting and she didn't give a fig if he noticed, either. She didn't like the soggy biscuit one bit, no matter how much her brother did and no matter how many knights adorned Albert's ancestry. His unwelcome offer for her last season only intensified her hostile feelings toward the man. If her brother hadn't loved her so well, she was sure she would have been handed to Albert Pedley and his withered fortune on a silver plate. She shivered at the thought.

A server came to their table and opened the wine. Gwendolyn shook off her frustrations and held out her glass to him, determined to have a memorable time on her holiday.

When the man made to pour out for Ellie, she covered the rim of wine glass with her fingertips.

"What's this? No wine for you, Ellie?" Weston teased.

Gwendolyn sighed. "You will have to excuse Ellie. Her mother insists that tea is the only civilized drink in the world."

"It's true, you know. Mama says the very reason Father—"

"Now, Ellie," Weston interrupted her, then offered to take the wine from the server—he never stood on ceremony when it came to his friends. The waiter relinquished the bottle and Weston gently removed Ellie's hand. He poured her a glass of the deep cherry-plum liquid. "There are people who have been consuming wine responsibly for centuries, and besides, your mama is not here." He grinned. "So you can have her share, as well." He passed the bottle to Albert who poured himself the rest of the wine, then handed the empty bottle to the server.

Ellie blushed and deflated some.

"Thank you, Weston. I'm going to make Ellie have a good time on this trip even if I expire from performing the task." Gwen took a sip of her wine.

"Then I shall do the same." Weston lifted his glass. "Here's to a good time." He winked at Ellie.

Gwendolyn's dearest friend raised her glass last, as if doing so would have sealed the bargain. All four glasses clinked delicately.

Ellie sipped from her drink, the liquid barely touching her lips. Her tongue darted out to sample the drop. "Mmm."

"You like it then, El?" Gwendolyn asked.

Ellie grinned as if proud of herself. "In a word, yes!" She nodded once for emphasis.

Weston leaned over to Ellie. "Just wait until you taste your second helping."

"Second?" She set her vessel down and looked over at Gwendolyn, her eyes gone wide again from behind her mask.

"Ellie." Gwendolyn leaned toward her friend. "You must relax. No one here is going to tattle on you, nor are they going to pass judgment on you for having a glass or two of wine."

Ellie slid her a doubtful look, nibbling on her lower lip.

"Darling, there is such a thing as being too sheltered in one's life."

"Now, Gwen, remember, Ellie is younger than you are—"

"Oh, Weston, stop being such a parent."

Weston shook his head and sighed.

Gwendolyn set her drink down and turned to face Ellie. "I see I'm going to have to instruct you on a few things."

"Here we go," Weston said under his breath. He scooped up his mask and after donning it, settled back into his seat.

Albert rose. "I can endure no more of this drivel. I'm going for a walk. I shall return for the first course." He nodded to Weston and left the table.

Ignoring Albert, she shot her brother a narrow-eyed glare and turned back to Ellie. "First of all, remove that silly piece of chiffon from your neckline." Gwendolyn leaned over to Ellie and stuck her fingers down the front of her dress. Ellie gasped as she did so. After fumbling around for a moment or two, Gwendolyn withdrew the fabric. "There. You see? Far more sophisticated." She dropped it like a used handkerchief.

Ellie glanced down at herself. She immediately made to cover her chest with her hands.

Gwendolyn caught Ellie's hands in hers. "I knew you would try that. Do you think these men have never seen a woman's décolletage before?"

Ellie opened her mouth, and as if she were unable to think of a suitable return, she pressed her lips together.

She relinquished her hold on Ellie. "Now, observe. No one in this room has even noticed now that your dress has joined the reasonably fashionable."

Weston shifted in his seat. "Gwen, perhaps Ellie is not at ease with a 'reasonably fashionable' neckline. Have you thought for one moment about her comfort?"

"Nonsense, Weston. What woman does not wish to be looked at by a man?"

Weston leaned over to Ellie and whispered loud enough for Gwen to hear, "This is what your mama warned you about." He indicated to his sister with a tilt of his head.

"Oh, Weston, stop, or you will frighten her to death."

Ellie's gaze dropped to the table. "Please do not fight over me. I will abide."

"Good. I knew you would. You will get used to men turning their attention to you, I promise." Dismissing her brother's heavily annoyed sigh, Gwendolyn patted Ellie's shoulder then reached for her drink.

Ellie reached for her wine as well and took a good-sized swallow.

"Now, just because we have masks on doesn't mean we can't flirt."

"Flirt?"

"Watch me now. I am going to take a turn round the room. See if you can tell when I'm flirting and with whom."

"Gwen, I hardly think —"

"Hush, Weston," she said as she stood. "Now remember, don't take your eyes off me, El."

"I, on the other hand, refuse to watch. There is a line of decorum no one should cross, just in case you hadn't noticed, sister, dear." His tone had turned mocking but his grin appeared devilish.

She harrumphed. "I have had enough teasing from you." She pushed feebly at the back of her brother's head as she passed by.

Gwendolyn extracted her fan from her reticule. As she walked slowly around the room, she toyed with the long, slender object, opening and closing it again, dangling it from its ribbon. Making a circle with her thumb and forefinger, she stroked it, letting her fingers slide from tip to hilt. She smiled and nodded at a few men, some even made to stand for her, but she kept walking, discouraging any further contact.

If Marcello hadn't seen the girl with his own eyes, he would have scoffed at the thought that such a beautiful creature would turn up at a Venetian ball. She belonged on Mount Olympus where the other goddesses gathered.

Nonetheless, she was flesh and blood.

She couldn't have been from this region, not with skin the color of fresh cream and hair that reminded him of honey warmed by the sun. Her mask allowed a hint of her allure to show, but he preferred a woman's face bare—to witness the sparkle in her eye, the rose tint of her cheek and the knowing tilt of her lips when she grinned. He imagined her shoulders and legs unclothed as well. And the rest of her…

"*Mio Dios*," he whispered.

His body stirred to life as he watched her dally with her fan. He'd do anything to have her hands slide up and down his cock in such a way.

He closed his eyes, picturing her wrapped like Caesar's mistress in his sheets. He would start at her toes and kiss his way up her legs. She'd giggle when he reached the backs of her knees—ah, the backs of a woman's knees. A place every man should explore with his lips and tongue at least twice a night. She would whimper and plead with him to continue higher, but he'd delay it as long as possible, drawing her need to the heated surface of her body. He'd bring her to the edge of passion until she could only sigh his name.

Perhaps he'd have a basket of blackberries next to the bed. He'd use the curve of her lower back as his plate and lap the berry juice from her soft skin—an enticing pastime to aspire to for certain, the possibilities of bed play with this alluring nymph were endless. And he longed to experience them all. His gaze swept over her.

He watched with the awareness of a hawk as she teased and tormented her audience. Every man in the room wanted her. However, no one but Marcello would lose himself between her thighs this night—of this he would make certain.

Oh, Yes. She would be in his arms at dawn, sated and drowsy from his lovemaking.

* * * *

"That was amazing," Ellie exclaimed when Gwendolyn returned to the table.

"Truly. And I'd better clean my pistols. Who knows how many rakes I'm going to have to call out now that you have beckoned every single man in the room to your attention?"

She reclaimed her seat and slid her brother a glance that called for his silence on the matter. She tucked her fan back into her reticule and turned to Ellie, "Now if I can do it, so can you."

Ellie shook her head in protest. "Not with strangers!"

Gwendolyn thought for a moment. "Very well, perhaps you can start simply. Weston?"

"What?" he asked, startled if not perturbed.

"I need you to let Ellie practice her wiles on you."

Chapter Three

"Practice her *what*?" Alarm coursed through Wes.

"You won't have to do a thing. Just sit there." Disallowing further protests from him, she stood and waved to Ellie to do so as well. "Now, I want you to walk by Weston and touch him as you go."

Ellie nodded. As she swept past Wes, she bumped the silk-draped pannier at her hip into his chair.

"No, no, El, not like that. Like this." Beginning a few paces from Weston, she let her forefinger slide all the way across his shoulders as she bypassed her brother.

Wes turned to Gwendolyn. "Oh, that was subtle."

Gwen huffed out a breath. "Very well, I will do it again." She spun on her heel and made a second pass, this time letting the outside of her forearm brush the silk strings of his mask. The ends of the ribbons softly skimmed the skin of Wes' neck on either side of his queue

He shivered.

"There," she said smugly, watching him over her shoulder.

"You tickled me." He scratched at the gooseflesh that stood up on his skin. "That doesn't count."

"It does indeed, my dear." Gwendolyn grinned. "I garnered a reaction from you."

"Let me try, Gwennie. I think I can do that." Ellie made her pass, but Wes didn't react. Ellie pouted and flopped back down into her chair.

"Not to worry, dearest. Weston was just prepared, that's all. Next time we'll catch him by surprise."

"I think not." He held up his hands. "I'm done playing the unwitting suitor."

"But—"

"I'm serious, Gwen. No more." He looked up to see the servers filing into the room, Albert following closely behind. "And besides, here is supper."

Gwendolyn patted her best friend on the hand and spoke in a hushed tone. "Don't you worry, my dear. I vow here and now to help you escape from the bubble of unnecessary protection your mother has blown around you."

Ellie's eyebrows knitted together as if she were in doubt that it was possible to do such a thing.

Winking at Ellie to assuage her apparent unease, Gwendolyn settled into her chair. She was determined to make this a trip neither of them would ever forget. Saving her friend from the rigors of society was first on her list, but in addition, Gwendolyn wanted to achieve a few new experiences for herself, and at her age, she was past due. However, in the back of her mind she wondered if her first kiss was too much to ask for.

Albert returned to his seat next to Ellie Appleton. He hadn't seen her since last season's disaster and thought she was developing quite nicely—unlike dear

Gwendolyn, whom he felt hadn't matured emotionally in the least.

Placing his napkin across his lap, he glanced over at the girls and compared the size of their breasts. Ellie's looked much more fluffy and ripe as opposed to Gwendolyn's seemingly tighter ones.

Last spring, when he'd heard from third and even fourth parties that Gwendolyn had adamantly refused his suit, it had angered him. Honestly, who did the Rawleighs think they were?

It occurred to him that both Gwendolyn and Wes were rigid, each in their own way. He'd wanted to be Wes' best friend for years, but Wes held other interests, most of which bored Albert out of his skull, effectively pushing him to the background. In a matter of weeks — upon the twin's birthday — Wes' name would be added to the Peerage Roll. Then, as iniquitous fate would have it, Wes would hold his father's Baronetcy in the palm of his spoiled hand.

Sir Weston Rawleigh.

Albert harrumphed. The bootlicking and scraping to get closer to Wes became staler every day. He should either find a way to make the Rawleighs warm up to him or abandon his quest for a branch on their family tree. Hell, once the decision was made to leap from the Rawleigh's lofty shrubbery, perhaps he'd land upon Ellie's generous body. Albert wondered idly if Miss Appleton had a dowry equivalent to her curves.

Ellie thought the meal divine, with each delectable course better than the last. Close to midnight, the entire gathering was escorted to a sumptuous ballroom, where a string quartet played from a dais in the corner. Groups of chairs — some with tables — were strewn around the room for those who wished to rest between sets. Weston had garnered one for their party from which to watch the festivities.

Soaking up the sights of the other guests in their beautiful evening wear, Ellie felt completely at ease. Gwendolyn had been correct about the masks. Not only could one's mask be as lavish as one wished, but hiding behind it was almost wicked. She suppressed a grin behind the pretense of a yawn at the thought.

Albert excused himself and stalked over to a row of empty chairs, far on the opposite end.

"That Albert and his ever-sour attitude," Gwendolyn scoffed then turned to Ellie. "How are you feeling, dear?"

Ellie untied her mask and let it fall from her face into her waiting hands. "Impec-ca-bully well," she replied, swallowing a hiccup, although her cheeks were rather warm and her entire body felt fuzzy from the inside out.

Gwendolyn pulled out a fan, and handed it to Ellie. "Make use of this, my dear. Your cheeks are practically on fire."

"Oh m' goodness." Ellie concentrated on taking the proffered item from Gwendolyn. However, she found the fan difficult to grasp the way the room seemed to oscillate. She grinned in triumph when she finally took up the fan.

"Poor Gwennie," Ellie commented to Weston, who had removed his mask as well. "She's had to watch out for me all even-ing. She hasn't had a single chance to find a handsome fore-igner to kiss. That's what she wants to do, you know. But I just want to wear pretty dresses and go sh-shopping." She eyed him with a tilt of her head and swept at her face with Gwendolyn's fan, grazing her nose in the process.

Gwendolyn leaned over to Ellie and whispered with a half-warning, "My dear, the wine seems to have loosened your tongue."

Weston glanced at Gwendolyn with a raised eyebrow and gently took the fan from Ellie. "Allow me."

Ellie leaned her cheek to Weston. "Thank you, Wes-n. That feels won-erful."

"You poor thing. What have I done, introducing you to the delights of the nectar of the gods and in such volume?" Weston murmured, gazing down at her.

Isn't he just the sweetest thing? "You are too kind."

"And you, my dear, are a bit tippled, aren't you?" His eyes sparkled.

"Perhaps we should take Ellie out for some air, Weston." Gwennie suggested.

"Yes, that's a fine idea." Placing the fan on the table, Weston stood then helped Ellie to her feet.

Gwendolyn took her other arm and in no time, they were awash in moonlight overlooking the Grand Canal.

"Isn't the view magnificent?" Gwennie sighed.

Weston made to move away from Ellie, but she slipped her hand around his waist and held on tightly. She wondered at the fact that she didn't want him anywhere but by her side, and refused to let him go, even for the sake of decorum. He was quite handsome in his evening clothes, and there was really no one else she wanted here with her.

Ellie risked a glance at Weston, and in that instant, even as she detected a spark of surprise in his eyes, she smiled at him.

Gwendolyn suddenly felt uncomfortable as if she were intruding upon a private moment between Ellie and Weston. She was about to say so when fingers closed around her elbow from behind.

"A dance, *Signorina*."

The deep Italian-accented male voice had stirred the ringlets next to her ear, causing a tickle that she had to resist scratching at with her gloved fingers. Gwendolyn turned to face the man. Dressed in black eveningwear, he was tall with broad shoulders. His leather commedia half-mask, a la *Pantalone*, sported bushy white eyebrows. Strange, but she had not seen him on her tour of the room earlier that evening. Surely she would have noticed someone as tall as Weston.

Before she could react, she was being led from the balcony to the center of the dance floor.

Gingerly stepping her way through the minuet, Gwen tried to steal glances at her partner, but his mask prevented her from even a glimpse of anything above his nose, which, in her estimation, was average in size. What were above average, and quite a ways, were his full lips and cleft chin, positioned flawlessly upon his strong masculine jaw. He danced well, thank goodness, but the heat of his hand through the fabric of their gloves disturbed her. Instead of warming her, it sent shivers that shimmered all the way up her arm. He absolutely radiated power.

His gaze seemed to snap to Gwendolyn's. He'd caught her staring at his face. She turned away, her cheeks afire beneath her mask. She heard him chuckle and she drew her lower lip between her teeth. He'd probably never had a more ill-mannered partner in all his days. It was then she realized that he was leading her out of the room, onto the balcony opposite from where Weston and Ellie were. A red flag unfurled in her mind, swishing before her eyes as if they were on a ship in a gale-force wind.

After turning a corner, Gwendolyn spoke up. "Er, *Signore*, I think it would be best if we—"

"Hush now, *mia ciliegia*." He pulled her into his arms. "I have been watching you all evening and I must help myself to a taste of your lips."

Gwendolyn felt her eyes widen beneath her mask. "Wha—?" She'd only gotten half of the word out before his mask swooped down to hers.

Wes was enjoying the feel of Ellie's arm pulling him close to her body, and yet admitted that it was rather odd. He'd not noticed before that she'd grown into a woman. At least, not that he could remember.

She was terribly sweet the way she looked up at him, her eyes shining and that silly half-drunken smile on her face. If they had met under different circumstances, he'd probably be kissing her right now.

His gaze dropped to her parted lips.

Good God. Wes abruptly turned his face toward the stone balcony railing. *What am I thinking?* He needed to get Ellie back to the table...back into the populated room and quickly, before he began spouting sonnets to her. They'd been friends for years, and he was certain Gwendolyn would do him a tremendous harm for even thinking about taking her best friend in his arms. The situation wasn't only befuddling, but dangerous as hell.

He turned back to the tempting young lady who clung to his side. "We should go back inside, Ellie."

With obvious reluctance, Ellie agreed. "Yes, I suppose we should."

Wes swallowed, and offered her his elbow, all too aware with a rapidly growing desire that he shared her disinclination.

When the man's warm lips touched Gwendolyn's cool ones, she inhaled sharply and pushed at his rock-hard shoulders, trying to escape, but it was no use. She might as well have been encased in amber. She had hoped to be a willing participant in the first kiss she received from a man, but this situation was intolerable. *How dare he take me in his solid, unrelenting and...* He held her gently within the protective wall of his arms. *The nerve of some...* His mouth slanted over hers. *And subject me to his demands...* His lips were more pliant than she'd originally thought. *His questionable demeanor...* He surrounded her like a luxurious, warm blanket. *His delightful scent.* Without thinking, Gwendolyn inhaled deeply once, twice, thrice.

"One should be careful what they wish for." She'd heard the voice as is someone had spoken the words from next to her. Hadn't this been exactly what she'd wanted to happen on this trip? The voice was indeed correct. *Fine then. I'll endure this as punishment for my over-optimistic outlook, then be done with it.*

Resigned to helplessness in his arms, she heard a sigh and a moment later realized that it had come from her. He was compelling—almost overwhelmingly so—and the cool evening breeze seemed to stir up and enhance his clean, spicy-herbal scent that engulfed her, made her dizzy.

He pulled away just enough to murmur, "I've seen the way you flit around your friend like a mother hen." He kissed her again then said just above a whisper, "and the way your body is crying out to be touched." He nipped at her bottom lip. "I am willing to provide you with amusements for the rest of the evening."

Good God! He thinks I'm looking for — She made to pull away but his arms tightened around her. "Release me this in —" Gwendolyn could not finish her tirade, for his mouth was covering hers in a way that demanded her silence.

The insolent man finally let her go, and she stumbled backward, her breath coming in harsh gasps until she found her footing. "How dare you?" her voice croaked like a toad but she didn't care.

He chuckled. "How dare I, *mia ciliegia*? Judging by the language your body has been speaking in that spectacular gown, you've been asking all night long to be stripped naked and laid out on a firm mattress." His gaze dove for a frantic heartbeat or two into the neckline of her dress.

Gwendolyn gasped. "You are vulgar, sir, and should have some sense slapped into you! I do *not* have to stand here and take your offensive behavior!" She spun on her heel and practically ran back to the ballroom.

She saw Ellie wave at her from across the room as she and Weston approached their table. Gwendolyn made straight away for her party.

"Did you find your foreign lover, Gwennie?" Ellie giggled.

"We are leaving," Gwen growled at her brother. When his eyebrows rose in question she snapped at him, "Now!" She reached for her fan and their cloaks.

"Very well, no need to get snippy." Weston waved a hand at the brooding Albert, and they all quit the *palazzo*.

* * * *

Marcello Verdante stood with his arms crossed over his chest. He leaned a hip against the railing of the front terrace at the *palazzo* where the first of many *Carnevale* celebrations was becoming a bore. Well, to be fair, the boredom began when his conquest for the evening had slipped from his grasp. Exactly how it had happened, he could not recall. He only knew he'd wanted her—the way she'd toyed with that fan of hers. He groaned.

As if sensing Marcello's tension, one of his men came to stand by his side. "Lucio, take Vas and follow that gondola." He jerked his chin toward the vessel that had just departed and was now heading in the direction of the Canale di San Marco. "Bring me any information you can on that woman. I shall be at my *palazzo* when you return."

"*Si, padrone*. The drunk one?"

"No, no. The *bella* with the honey-colored hair." *And the magnificent pomegranate lips.*

Chapter Four

When Ellie sat next to Wes in the gondola and reclined into his arms, his eagerness to accommodate her overrode whatever societal restrictions would have applied to a mere man and a woman. Chaperones, after all, were supposed to take into consideration not just the safety and care of their charges, but also see to their comfort. Wes thought Ellie looked so content in the moonlight, resting her head on his chest. He glanced up at Gwen. "She's been asleep since we sat down," he whispered, stroking a hand across her upper back.

Gwen gave him a tight-lipped smile which he promptly shrugged off as she turned her gaze out over the water.

Albert cleared his throat and nudged Wes. "I think we're being followed."

"Nonsense, Albert. This is *Carnevale*—there are hordes of people milling about, hobnobbing and whatnot. There isn't anywhere safer in the world than where we are right here, at this very moment."

Albert grunted in response and continued to peer around the legs of the gondolier.

Wes was taken aback at how little he cared about the happenings of the ancient celebration.

Ellie stirred in his arms and settled closer to him. After a moment she issued forth a precious sigh that caused the breath to flee his lungs. He caught himself before he hugged her closer and glanced over at his sister. Gwen seemed lost in her own little world.

He hadn't been in Venice for a full day and night, and Wes had never felt happier. A contented mood filled his being that, perhaps on this now-modified trip, he might uncover mysteries – not about where he visited, but about himself. His gaze came to rest once again on Ellie. She was practically in his lap. Pleased to no end, he dipped his head down and hid his grin in her fragrant hair. He knew it was risky to even think about letting his imagination run wild about Ellie. Regardless, he continued to coddle her as if she were his pet, a precious little dark-haired, blue-eyed bunny. What did it matter, really, pretending for the moment that Ellie was his pet? It was a sweet dream he could tuck away for a more private moment – a fantasy that perhaps a darling of a girl just like her would consent to be his. But would he ever be able to recreate these intense emotions with someone else? Could he find a woman that would make him feel important, needed…like a man instead of a boy?

Gwendolyn huffed out an agitated breath and clutched the front of her cloak closed. She pressed her lips together, remembering the feel of the stranger's mouth on hers. She shuddered. He could have done some serious damage to her virtue, not to mention her reputation with his strength, if anyone she knew had seen them in each other's arms. Relieved that she'd been masked the whole time, she resolved to place the gown she wore that night at the bottom of her trunk and never wear it again, lest someone recognize it from this evening. She'd have to arrange her hair differently. Perhaps she'd purchase a powdered wig.

"Why are you scowling, Gwen?" Weston asked from next to her, bringing her out of her reverie.

"No reason," she snapped, then sent him a placating smile.

"Well," he murmured after a moment, "I'll not press you for information. Perhaps all you need is a good night's sleep."

"Yes, I'm quite sure that's the solution." None of her family or friends could ever know what liberties she'd allowed a perfect stranger tonight.

* * * *

Back at *Signore* Bernardo's palazzo, Gwendolyn unlocked the door for Weston. She then crossed to the window, tossing open the curtains to allow the moonlight to spill into the room.

Weston carried Ellie over to her bed. "I'll go ahead and tuck her in."

"Thank you, dear. I'm going for a walk, I'll be back soon." She untied her mask and tossed it onto her bed.

"No, Gwen. Wait for me. I'll only be a moment," he said, slipping off Ellie's shoes and tossing them aside.

"That won't be necessary. You said yourself we're safe here in Venice, remember? Now I shan't be long and besides, I'm only going for a short turn round Piazza San Marco." She flipped the hood of her cloak up, spun on her heel and headed out of the door.

"Gwendolyn, wait!" he hollered to her, struggling to hastily cover Ellie as the door shut behind the ever obstinate Gwendolyn.

Ellie moaned and unsuccessfully tried to turn over onto her belly.

Forgetting about his irritating sister for the moment, Wes gritted his teeth as he looked down at Ellie, her brunette curls cascading over her pillow. His playful thoughts from earlier that evening made his and Ellie's close proximity in the quiet room most hazardous.

She tugged at the top of her bodice in her sleep. He supposed it would be uncomfortable for anyone to sleep in a woman's trappings.

"This is the first and last time I offer to put a woman to bed that I'm not seriously planning on bedding myself," he grumbled. He unhooked her stomacher, removed her skirts and slid her silk sleeves from her arms. After unfastening her panniers, he set them aside, but left her corset, stockings and pantalets on.

The air departed from his lungs when he noticed her creamy breasts pushing up over the tight corset. Ellie looked delectable. She'd probably not like to sleep in the contraption society deemed proper. Intending to loosen it for her, he held his breath as he slid his fingers down the front of it.

Ellie made a sound that was part groan, part sigh.

Wes swallowed.

Her skin was soft and pliable, and Wes's cock was rapidly becoming the opposite. *Keep your mind on your work, man,* he scolded himself. Grinding his teeth together, he only undid the first few hooks of the busk then removed his trembling hand. *There. That should be enough for comfort's sake.*

He calmed considerably when his task was complete and he quit the room.

A walk would be a good idea, as his ardor had not yet cooled. Moreover, he needed to catch up with Gwendolyn before she got herself into some real trouble.

At the bottom of the stair case he ran into Albert.

"You up for a drink, Wes? There are a dozen or so bottles of wine left over from *Signore* Bernardo's party." He tipped his head toward a table in the corner of the grand parlor.

Even though his friend had inquired with a bit more joviality than he'd displayed all evening long, Wes was preoccupied with finding his sister. "Er, have you seen Gwen? She must have passed by here a not five minutes ago," he asked, scanning the room.

"No, I have not," he murmured, quite obviously disappointed in the change of topic.

Once again diverted from his purpose, Wes took his friend's unenthusiastic response into consideration and sympathized with him. "I'm sorry, Albert. I know how you two don't get along."

Albert shrugged a shoulder and looked away, as if he did not wish to speak on it.

"Come now. You knew she'd be here, so why did you agree to the holiday?"

"Quite honestly, I don't know why, Wes." He let out a pent-up breath. "Perhaps, I was hoping she had matured a bit since last season."

Weston recalled how last year, before Albert had officially presented his offer to their mother, he had hinted to Wes that he was interested in his sister. But when Wes mentioned it to Gwendolyn, she made such a fuss that everyone in town became aware of how she felt. "Again, I apologize. She's just—"

"Spoiled? Childish? Troublesome?"

Wes grinned and slapped Albert good-naturedly on the back. "I get your meaning, Albert. Let's not beat a dead horse, shall we?"

Albert shrugged, which for him was as good as compliance.

"Tell you what, come take the night air with me and then we'll return and drink the house dry." Wes smiled, purposefully leaving out the fact that he wanted to keep an eye on Gwen.

"That would suit me fine," Albert said with a nod. "The first round's on me."

He chuckled at the jest.

* * * *

Ellie woke with a start. She was alone in the room, but the fringes of a naughty dream still hovered at the edge of her consciousness. Her skin still felt heated and between her legs moisture had gathered. When she skimmed her hand down over her pantalets at the juncture of her thighs, she realized that her dress had been stripped away. When did that happen? Had Gwennie given her assistance?

She sighed with relief. Her darling Gwennie. A better friend couldn't be found. Even though Gwennie was the daughter of a Baronet, she'd insisted on treating Ellie like an equal—regardless of the Appleton family's lack of status. What would she do without her best friend to assist and guide her through life? Gwennie's instruction helped her more than any big sister could have.

She loved to hear Gwennie's wicked words about lovers and men. Why, it fairly made her tremble. She furtively longed to be kissed by a man, to have his hands on her. It was her deepest, darkest secret, one she wouldn't even allow herself to think on it when someone else was in the same room with her. Mercy, even her mama didn't talk about such things.

The only conclusion she could reach was that to long for such stimulation was so evil, so perilous, it was a sin to even speak of. She knew how to make babies, everyone did, but oh, how her mind and body wanted to know how a man's skin felt against hers.

Sometimes at night she would pretend that her pillow was a handsome man, and she'd play that he was kissing her. Almost always she'd slip her hand between her legs — the heat of her fingers making her squirm with desire. If she made herself feel that way, who knew what a man was capable of doing to her? She nearly swooned at the thought.

Ellie admitted to herself that she needed to feel that pleasure right here and now — and she'd have to do it quickly before Gwennie returned. Quickly untying her pantalets, she then reached down between her folds and closed her eyes, allowing the bliss-like sensation to flow over her.

* * * *

Regardless of the bustling *Carnevale* crowd, Venice was a beautiful city. As Gwendolyn strolled along the shimmering Venetian Lagoon, on the right stood the Doge's private residence, a five-hundred year-old Gothic palace in which the Doge himself, Lodovico Manin, resided.

She paused to gaze upon the structure as if to memorize it. She admired the intricate brickwork that made the building's façade one of the most recognized edifices in Italy.

At once, her hood was pulled down over her face. She drew in a breath to protest when the thought flitted through her mind that it was likely some drunken reveler behaving inappropriately. Her positive feelings fled, however, when a cloth sack came down over her head and she was unceremoniously lifted from the ground.

Gwendolyn was unable to scream, so tight was the hold on her ribcage. She kicked her legs until they were restrained at the ankles, then tried to escape by twisting at the waist, but still her efforts were thwarted.

Suddenly, she was set down on a hard surface, and to her horror, her captives held her there by practically sitting on her. She was sure to pass out as her chest was being restricted under some terrible weight. The blackness slowly became pleasant as she slipped into unconsciousness.

* * * *

"*Il mio Dio*, what have you two done?" Marcello gaped at the mass of fabric on the settee his men had just dumped there.

"We brought you the girl, as you requested," Lucio remarked, indicating the settee as Vas stripped the cloth bag from his victim.

Marcello groaned. "I did not ask you to bring me the girl—only *information*!"

Vas glanced at Lucio, his shoulders drooping in exasperation.

"*Madonamia*." Marcello raked a hand through the top of his hair. "Did anyone see you?"

"No, *padrone*, I made sure. However, had I left it up to Lucio, he would have sent invitations for the viewing."

"Shut your mouth, Vas," Lucio growled. "Everyone makes mistakes."

"Not nearly as many as you do."

"Enough, you two! You fight as if you were related." Marcello took a deep breath and sighed. "Leave us."

After Lucio and Vas had quit the room, Marcello lifted the girl and laid her on a deep, cushioned window seat that overlooked the Grand Canal. It was a stunning view from the fourth floor of his rented *palazzo*, but he didn't have time to admire it at the moment. He needed to figure out what to do with his unwitting guest.

He sat down next to her, unclasped her cloak, then smoothed the hair from her porcelain, maskless face. She was even more beautiful lying there unconscious than she had been at the ball where she flaunted her wares like a common courtesan. He'd fully expected her to steal away with him for a night of pleasure, but when she had struggled in his arms during a simple kiss, he realized that she'd only been stretching her wings. Still, he needed to know more about her. His gaze dropped to her curvy, white décolletage, and he moistened his lips with a sweep of his tongue. There was no doubt in his mind that she was an untried maiden, but there was something in her manner that told him she might be open to sampling a few carnal pleasures. And he was just the man to show her the way.

But he was no pervert to amuse himself with her body while she was oblivious to his presence. Nor could he chance being recognized by anyone. He rose and stepped over to a sideboard where he poured himself a healthy draft of sweet vermouth. After refastening his mask that he'd removed once he'd arrived home, he tossed half his drink back and returned to the window seat.

"I think it is time you woke up, *Signorina*," he said, running his knuckle down her cheek.

She groaned.

The sound made his blood surge within his veins. He wanted to be the one to draw that sound from her lips, over and over again until she came by means of his hands, his fingers, his tongue—

Her eyelids fluttered open, and his breath caught in his throat at the glimpse of her stunning green eyes in the moonlight. He stood, placing himself in shadow.

Gwendolyn's head pounded terribly. She touched her cool fingers to her temples. "Where am I?" She gasped and sat upright, at once remembering the frightening way in which she had been transported to where she now found herself. The throbbing in her head echoed her own beating heart. She swayed and nearly tipped backwards.

Something soft yet strong steadied her. When she looked about to see what or who had helped her, she observed a man slip into the shadows away from the moonlight.

"It is all right, *Signorina*. Do not fret."

She recognized the deep, accented voice from the ball. She drew back upon the window seat as if he were assaulting her.

"You have no need to fear me. Just relax."

"Why have you brought me here? Where am I? Who are you? What do you want?" She spoke over the dull ache behind her eyes but could not make out the obscure figure who purposefully kept himself from the light. The full moon shone so brightly, it was if Gwendolyn was sitting in the center of a pillar of illumination, barely able to see beyond it.

The man chuckled. "Your questions will be answered, *mia delicato ciliegia*, but only if you are patient."

"Patient? You almost killed me when you brought me here! God knows what evil you have planned."

He smiled in the darkness. She could almost make out his white teeth. "Had I planned anything immoral for you, you would already feel the after-effects, I assure you."

His voice was rich with dubious promises. Heat rose to Gwendolyn's cheeks. Her gaze dropped to her lap.

"What is your name?" His tone was in no way rude, but clearly commanding.

Looking up startled, she shot back, "What is yours?"

"You can either tell me your name or I will find out for myself. The choice is yours."

"It's Miss Rawleigh. Miss Gwendolyn Rawleigh."

Gwendolyn waited for him to introduce himself. When he didn't, she prodded. "Sir, it is customary to give one's name in return for one which has been offered." She could hear him breathing, and it sent a shiver down her spine, unnerving her like nothing ever had. "Forgive me. You must not be as civilized as you claim to be," she commented with feigned flippancy, attempting to cover her tremor.

"This is *Carnevale, Signorina* Rawleigh," he indicated with a sweep of his hand. "I never give my name during *Carnevale*."

"Why?" the question was out before she could stop it. What did she care if he refused to give her his name?

"At *Carnevale*, you can gamble, drink and do any manner of things without being held responsible for your actions — provided no one knows it's you."

Gwendolyn exhaled through her nose. "Well, you must be more debauched than I originally assumed, for only a criminal would feel the need to hide from the world as you do."

At once, he seized her wrists and dragged her from the light into darkness. His body pressed intimately to hers, backing her up against the wall. "My birth does not make me a criminal, *Signorina*." His voice sounded soft and demanding at the same time. "Nor does my decision to keep my situation a secret. Neither of these things are any of your concern. What you should be concerned with are the thoughts going through my mind of the delicious things I want to do to your body."

"How dare—" her protest burst out in the form of a breathless plea just as his lips came down on hers.

Chapter Five

Gwendolyn once again found herself in a position where she was not a willing participant. Although he had not hurt her in any way, she was still distraught. *Who is he and why did he bring me here? What is he going to do with me?* It was at that moment her sense of smell recognized his clean, herbal scent. She wrestled with the memory of his stirring first kiss, but his lips seemed to be telling their own version of the tale. He kissed her as if they'd been engaged for months.

Slowly, the grip he had on her wrists melted into warmth. Gwendolyn abandoned her struggle and clung to him. The fact that she could almost fancy enjoying his attentions invaded her thoughts. No one knew where she was, not even herself. The situation should certainly have sounded an alarm in her head, but for some reason it didn't. It made things easier.

He pulled away just enough to whisper against her lips. "That is much better, *mia ciliegia.*"

She didn't open her eyes when he spoke. And whatever that word meant, the word he kept using when referring to her, sent a thrill over her skin that penetrated to her very center. Gwendolyn's jaw went slack as she allowed the sensation to ripple through her body. Her lips were once again being softly teased by his, and when his tongue touched hers, she gasped at the feeling. Shyly she mimicked him, stroking, caressing. By example, he showed her how to worship his lower lip and she followed dutifully.

"Ah, yes, this is how I want you—soft and willing, eager to learn," he breathed and trailed kisses across her cheek, down her neck and back up toward her ear.

"Learn?" Gwendolyn repeated languidly, tilting her head to grant him greater access.

"As you teach your friend how to flirt, I shall teach you other more serious pleasures, and you will find out from me where all your flirting is supposed to lead."

His wicked promise had been whispered very close to her ear. She'd heard every word, but the gooseflesh crawling along her arms and down her back prevented her from responding with even a minuscule measure of intelligence. She felt a strange tingling at the tips of her breasts which only happened once in a while late at night, when a wicked thought crept into her mind.

"W-what sort of things would you be teaching me?" she asked, nearly breathless. Gwendolyn knew she shouldn't have inquired, but she couldn't help herself.

He pulled away from her neck and dropped down. He rose, his hands filled with fistfuls of her skirts. Gwendolyn gasped as panic began to well within her, but there was nowhere to run. He flung the fabric out of the way to rest his palms beneath her panniers on her hips. The only thing between his skin and hers were her thin pantalets. Gwendolyn's heart pounded in her ears. His touch simmered across her skin and she thought she might squirm from the heat. They slid around to her backside and lifted her from the ground. She was now chest to chest with him, hip bone to hip bone. He splayed his fingers across her bottom as if measuring the expanse.

Yes, her body pleaded. Her mind, however, remained misty.

Something rigid pressed against her in a most intimate way, almost — but not quite — touching her in a place that suddenly seemed most eager to be engaged. Gwendolyn tilted her pelvis forward and whatever it was that wanted access to her now had it. At once, she realized the firm item was his manhood, and it made her dizzy to think how close he was to her. She was sure to burn in hell for acting so wanton, but lord, the overwhelming feeling was...heady, tantalizing, and *terribly* naughty.

He made a sound, somewhere between a moan and a growl, and at once she was on her feet being led to a settee across the room, well away from the light of the window. They sat, and he leaned into her, causing her to recline the rest of the way onto the bench. His hands made their way beneath her skirts again and before she could protest, his lips met hers in a searing kiss.

Gwendolyn turned her face away, desperate to draw breath, but his wonderful scent threw her already foggy mind into a spin. Not two heartbeats later, he found the slit between the legs of her pantalets. He murmured something in Italian, and, as if obeying his nearly unspoken command, her knees spread, her most private place seeking his touch.

"*Si*, that's it. God, I haven't even touched you yet, and you're soaked," he whispered.

He strummed his digits over her excited flesh, Gwendolyn's wordless exclamation echoed in the room. She felt swollen and hot beneath his touch. God, if he would do that just a bit harder…. She had no rational reason to want it so, but she had to have it. Her breathing turned ragged, and she tilted her hips, lifting herself toward his rhythmic petting. She squeezed her eyes shut, as if her body knew she needed to concentrate.

"Mmm, that must be good for you. Your pearl is so rigid, so demanding under my fingers," he murmured and applied more pressure to the sensitive spot.

The combination of his titillating discourse and his hand made her cry out as something utterly sublime happened to her body. She shuddered helplessly as overpowering waves washed over her.

He pressed his knuckles to her, barely moving them in unison with her hips. "You are so beautiful when you come *mia dolce ciliegia*," he whispered, his lips grazing her earlobe with every word.

Gwendolyn opened her eyes. Her flesh was so sensitized now she could no longer bear his intimate touch. Wrapping her hands around his big strong wrist, she attempted to disengage contact.

He chuckled. "Had enough for tonight?"

To her great mortification, Gwendolyn's only answer was an involuntary gulp of air.

"Very well." He removed his hands. Smoothing both palms over her legs and pausing when he came in contact with the hard shivering muscles of her thighs, he applied gentle pressure, rubbing as he went, until the quivering stopped.

A small moan escaped from between her lips at his gentle succor.

He helped her to stand and settled her skirts back over her panniers.

Gwendolyn attempted to control her quaking. Her legs had been terribly weakened by the wondrous activity as she waited at the foot of the settee while he retrieved her cloak from the window seat. His black silhouette against the moonlit window made her stomach shudder. He seemed bigger than life, taller than she had remembered. His shoulders practically filled the space. When he walked back to her with her cape, she had to tilt her face back to try to find anything beyond his mask that would set her mind at ease, but to no avail. He was a faceless stranger who had nudged open a door that she'd had no business stepping through. Once again, as it always had in her life, her curiosity conquered proper etiquette. But never had it gone so far. She was equally angry at herself as she was with him.

At her throat he fastened the gold clasp and smoothed her hair back. "Shall we carry on with your lessons tomorrow night?"

"Sir, I cannot continue in this manner," she said with finality, attempting to keep her voice steady.

"Why? Did you not enjoy your experience?"

Gwendolyn felt her cheeks ignite. Her embarrassment coupled with the reality of what she'd just done — what she'd allowed him to do to her had reached an intolerable level. "It's not that. I was curious and you… You satisfied my inquisitiveness. That is all." She glanced around in search of an exit route.

He stepped forward and pulled her into his arms "Are you not craving more at this very moment?" His deep voice rolled over her like dark, threatening rain clouds.

Gwendolyn gasped as he read the very thoughts she refused to admit she harbored.

He slid his hand down her back and caressed her bottom through the fabric of her skirts. "There are more delights of the flesh to explore," he said against her ear. "I know extensive ways in which to pleasure you, to bring you to heights you could have never imagined on your own."

Trying to nudge out of his arms she protested. "No, sir. I will not allow you to pursue me for such matters. I have other affairs to attend to—" Gwendolyn clamped her lips shut, hoping he didn't catch her accidental insinuation

"I am your only affair."

To her utter shame, he did notice. "I didn't mean—"

"There is no need to argue. I will find you," he said, while at the same time, escorting her to the door.

Looking for the words to object to his campaign, Gwendolyn sputtered all the way across the floor until she felt the hood of her cloak being lifted and placed over her head. The flower sack was once again employed, pinning her arms to her sides.

"Truly, there is no need to—"

"Ah, but there is. I cannot allow you to discover where you have been tonight and in turn, no one will be able to extract the information from you. As I said, I will find you."

Information? What on earth – ?

Gwendolyn felt herself being led away, down several flights of stairs and into a boat.

Marcello watched from his window as Vas and Lucio took Gwendolyn Rawleigh away in the gondola. His cock was maddeningly stiff, and it seemed to scream for release. He was in awe of what had occurred. He should have let her go, should have apologized from the first and told Vas and Lucio to take her back.

But she was far too tempting.

He closed his eyes. She had been like clay at the mercy of his hands, a willing pupil of his newfound calling as master of the sensual arts—and she had come so effortlessly by his fingers. He swore a string of words his mother would have chastised him for. Under normal circumstances, he'd never have thought of something like this, but when she was in his arms, his mind became blurry and he readily agreed to take on the impromptu position.

Miss Rawleigh had passed her first exam merely by her curiosity which would help her immensely with the forthcoming instruction he'd promised her. But why toy with her like this? What purpose would it serve? It wasn't as though he'd find any release in her virgin flesh.

Marcello swallowed at the idea, his groin giving a jerk as if eager to prove the thought false. If her curiosity could be coaxed anew, or if he could whet her interest, so to speak, he'd be buried deep within her before the close of *Carnevale*. He growled and pushed away from the window. For now, he'd have to take care of himself.

Gwendolyn stood still and counted to one hundred with her eyes shut tightly, just as the men had instructed. Even after she'd finished, she remained in the place they'd left her, the wind whipping her cloak about her legs. She took notice of the laughter of revelers as they bypassed her frozen position. With great effort, Gwendolyn relaxed her shoulders and slowly opened her eyes. She was once again in front of

Signore Bernardo's palazzo in which Ellie and her brother abided and where she could safely spend the rest of the evening—perhaps even the remainder of her trip. Tempted to turn her head toward the canal, she decided at the last moment not to, in case her former captors could still be seen.

Her body still hummed from the experience she'd had. As much as she should have been running for her life, she was pressed to admit that he really hadn't hurt her—scared her, yes, but not hurt her. He could have done much more damage, she was sure. He could have ravished her beyond repair, but he hadn't. Nor did his two thugs molest her in any irreparable way.

A breeze rustled the fabric of her cloak again and she tilted her head back in appreciation of the harmless caress. He had been quite skilled at what he'd done to her body, and when he told her there was more, the flesh between her legs had twitched at the thought.

Gwendolyn snapped out of her sinful reflection. This whole scenario was immoral, improper and decidedly impossible for a woman of her society to tolerate.

She focused again on the entrance to the palazzo, willing her feet to take her over the threshold.

A sigh of relief escaped her throat as she pushed her hood from her head and entered the opulent parlor.

Heading straight for the stairs, she glanced across the vast, richly decorated, common sitting room to where a handful of revelers had gathered, sprawled across padded chairs and comfortable-looking settees, when someone laughed heartily.

"Gwen?" Her brother's familiar voice called to her from the circle of divans. She stopped and turned toward him, praying that he could not read in her eyes where she'd been, or more importantly, what she'd been doing.

He stood and walked toward her. "God's teeth, have you been out and about since you left your room?"

Gwendolyn cleared her throat of emotion. "Yes, I have. But don't you worry yourself about it. I am going upstairs now and will see you tomorrow for breakfast." She turned and reached for the thick marble balustrade when he stopped her.

"Are you all right? You look a mess. Where have you been all this time?"

She turned to him and smiled. "I was out—walking. The wind whips something awful, off the canals." She chuckled nervously and patted the back of her hair into place, which probably didn't help in the least.

"Gwen," his voice held a warning but she quelled what certainly would turn into an inquiry.

"I am tired now. I will see you tomorrow." She reached out, patted his arm and continued up the stairs.

Weston forced out an audible breath that Gwendolyn ignored

.

Chapter Six

Gwendolyn spread jam onto a roll as she sat by herself on a terrace that afforded a lovely prospect of the Canale di San Marco, remembering her dreams of the night before. Exceedingly depraved dreams, they were. She would have sworn that in the midst of one of those dreams her private parts did that thing again, where her body shivered all over with pleasure, leaving her breathless and sated. It was delicious and maddening, all at the same time.

She shifted in her seat then glanced up to see her brother approach.

"Did you sleep well, Gwen?"

Gwendolyn cleared her throat. "I did. And you?"

"Once I got to sleep. I spent some time searching for you in Piazza San Marco before Albert and I retired to the parlor. I didn't want to make a fuss about it in front of him when you returned last night."

Gwendolyn detected the irritation in his voice and made to assuage his anger immediately. "I'm so sorry to have inconvenienced you. I was enjoying myself so much that I'd almost lost my way." She wasn't about to admit that he'd been right about her needing a chaperone.

"I thought as much." Weston let loose a sigh. "You *must* allow me to go with you next time. I'm on holiday, too, after all. In fact" — he smirked — "upon my return, Albert and I sat up until all hours drinking and socializing."

Relieved he'd absolved her of her sin from the night before, Gwendolyn made a face when Weston's companion was mentioned. She took a bite of her roll. "Hm," was all the reaction she'd give her brother regarding his friend.

Weston sighed as if disregarding Gwendolyn's perturbation regarding Albert. He looked about. "Where is Ellie?"

Gwen took a sip of her tea. "Ellie had an awful headache, so I told her to stay abed until she felt better."

Weston was quiet for a moment. "I feel responsible for her pain. After all, it was I who filled her wine glass innumerable times at supper last night."

Gwendolyn watched as her brother considered the situation, his eyebrows pinching together over the bridge of his nose.

"Gwen, before I venture forth, I should like to go see her. Do you mind waiting for me?"

"Go see Ellie, Weston, and take your time. I will be visiting shops that I'm sure you will not be interested in."

"My dear, I'd rather not have you running thither and yon by yourself in a strange city. We don't want a repeat of last night's adventure."

Gwendolyn rolled her eyes at him. *If only he knew.* "My dear Weston. It's *Carnevale*, and besides, your annoying tone is punishment enough, I assure you."

She popped the rest of her roll into her mouth, and chased it down with a sip of tea.

When she set her cup down, Weston took her by the hand. "Gwen, I know you don't like to hear it, but someday, someone is going to misinterpret your actions and assume you are something you're not." His words were emphasized with a tilt of his dark blond head toward her and a rising of eyebrows over his penetrating green eyes.

A bitter laugh echoed in her mind as if mocking her that Weston's scenario had already come to fruition. "You worry over much, my dear. I am perfectly capable of handling any and all situations." She smiled at him to cover her agitated nerves.

Besides, she was quite confident that the man, whoever he was, would not be able to find her. She'd planned her day and wardrobe perfectly. She was to wear her black wool cloak and hood, and hold a *Moretta* mask to her face between her teeth by a small wooden knob. Not only would she not be seen, but her voice wouldn't be heard, either. There was no chance of being recognized this way, and therefore, there was no way she would be bothered by that rake who chose not to give her his name.

"But, I do worry. It is my job as your brother to do so. And just in case you don't recall, I am supposed to act as your chaperone, not to mention that I am the man of the house since Father died."

"Yes, yes," Gwen waved a hand in dismissal of the subject. "Now, go on up and see Ellie. Just be sure you do not speak too loudly, and do not open the curtains. Her eyes are sensitive to the light this morning." She handed him the key to her and Ellie's room.

Wes sighed at being dismissed like an annoying fly. He stood and placed the key into the watch pocket of his waistcoat. He then picked up a pitcher of water and a stack of linen napkins from a sideboard that had remained from last night's impromptu amusement. "You are going to be the death of me, Gwen."

A bark of laughter erupted from Gwendolyn. "Now you truly sound like Mama."

Wes wrinkled his nose at her in frustration, and headed for Ellie's bedside.

As he ascended the stairs, he slowed. What was his real motivation for seeking Ellie out? It was almost as if a still small voice in the back of his mind had turned sour and was now nagging at him to confess that he possessed an evil intent for her, which was completely untrue.

Yes, he had nearly kissed Ellie last night on that balcony, but today — today he honestly and with all his heart wished to set his conscience at ease and apologize for being the cause of this morning's illness.

Wes rolled his gaze across the ceiling, disappointed in himself and his lack of willpower. He reached Ellie's door, entered and set the water and linens down, instantly noting the dark, restful, even sensual tone of the room. This visit could be very dangerous if he didn't keep his wits about him.

Ellie heard someone milling about the chamber and assumed it was Gwendolyn having forgotten something. "Gwennie?" she whispered.

"No, Ellie, it is I, Weston."

"Oh," she said softly. "What are you doing here?" She peeked at him through barely parted eyelids.

"Well, I felt badly about you being ill and wanted to offer whatever curative efforts I can to make you more comfortable," he whispered.

"That is terribly sweet of you, Weston, but shouldn't you be out enjoying this wonderful city instead of staying indoors playing nursemaid to an old sot"

He smiled, as if trying not to laugh. "You are anything but an old sot, my dear."

"Not from where I sit. Or in my case, lie," she murmured drolly.

"Silly girl." Weston grinned. "Do you mind if I apply an old remedy to help you through your suffering?"

Ellie smiled weakly. "Do your worst, sir."

"Very well. Now don't go away," he said, and moved to where her wash basin was.

Ellie heard the tinkling of water as it splashed about.

"I'm going to have to sit next to you. You don't mind, do you?"

Without a word, Ellie scooted over to accommodate him and closed her eyes, trusting him completely. The mattress dipped as he situated himself next to her. It felt intimate for Weston to actually be sitting next to her on the bed, but regardless, she relished the thought. In moments, his fingers were sweeping across her forehead, they were soft, and his action was so caring she almost smiled. A cool cloth came to rest over her eyes and she sighed.

"All right." Weston took one of her hands in his own. "I read about this in a book somewhere, the ancient Chinese used to do this to cure headaches." He pinched the skin and muscle between her thumb and index finger.

"Ouch!" Ellie tried to pull her hand from his.

"Good God! I'm so sorry, Ellie. I didn't mean to cause you additional pain," he said franticly. At once, he pressed his lips against the palm of her hand where his fingers had been.

Ellie froze.

So did Weston.

With her free hand, she gently pulled the cloth from her eyes to gaze on him in the dim light of the room. He was watching her with a look on his face she had never seen before. His mouth lingered over her skin, his breath warmed her palm.

Ellie swallowed, her heart making a leap within her chest.

When Weston leaned down and placed his lips on hers, the wet cloth dropped from her hand onto the floor. Her eyes closed dreamily all by themselves. She could feel the pleasant warmth seep all the way down her body, through to her very soul.

Mentally cursing himself, Wes vowed this was not what he'd intended for his ill friend… But damn it all, Ellie's were the most yielding lips he had ever kissed. Somewhere, deep in a fantastical part of his mind, he knew this was how she would be.

Wes brushed his mouth back and forth over her lips, luxuriating in their softness. She smelled of perfume and powder. Utterly feminine.

He cringed. That horrid voice was back again, trying to remind him that this was his sister's best friend, and he should not be taking advantage of her like this. The voice was without a doubt correct, but his body wholeheartedly rebelled against the idea of bringing the plundering of this sweet, darling girl to a screeching halt and quitting the room. The fact was he'd be inclined to stay the rest of the day like this, if she did not eject him from her sight first.

A small moan sounded from the back of her throat, which told him that she, too, was disposed to exploring this intriguing new pastime with him.

Without thinking, he stretched out next to Ellie on the bed and kissed a trail across her cheek. Ellie's breathing had gone ragged, so he happily occupied himself with kissing her neck. He felt her hand slip into his hair, and he groaned.

He moved lower, nudging the edge of her coverlet with his nose to kiss just beneath its satin boarder. He knew kissing the creamy swell of her breasts might lead him to more pleasurable planes, but he promised himself right then and there that when his lips met the top of her corset, he'd stop.

Wes moved lower and with a snap of his wrist, tossed her cover to the floor.

Ellie gasped and Wes did the same as he encountered her bare chest. She tried to cover herself with her hands as much as possible, but her nipples peeked out from between her splayed fingers. His cock surged at the sight of her holding her own breasts.

"Ellie," he breathed, taking in the view. "Where is your corset?"

"Over on the settee," she panted and indicated it with a tilt of her head. "I took it off earlier this morning."

"My God," he whispered, his eyes caressing her skin with a look that was sure to cause her to burst into the same flaming heat that engulfed him.

"Weston," she breathed, "don't stop."

He glanced up and saw the passion in her eyes just before she laid her head back onto the pillow, her hands sliding from her chest, down her abdomen and came to rest on her hips.

"Oh, Ellie," he groaned. He'd have to take this slow, lest she recognize what they were doing and put a stop to it.

And what are you doing? That damned voice inside Wes' head demanded.

Making love to Ellie, he answered and stroked his hand between the valley of her breasts, watching with hungry eyes as her soft flesh quivered.

Weston! the voice persisted.

Shut up, he countered. And at last, the nagging voice fell silent.

Wes caressed and gently kneaded her breasts until her breaths were issuing forth the sweetest sighs he'd ever heard.

"Do you like that?" Wes's tone was husky with dark excitement.

"In a word," she gasped, "yes," her voice high-pitched and terribly eager.

There she was, encouraging him again. How could he disappoint her? Wes leaned up on an elbow and began kissing her exposed chest, flicking his tongue out every so often to lap at her tender skin. *God, she sounds like she is going to come*, he thought as he listened to her rhythmic sighs. *She will. I'll make sure she does.* He grinned, then his mouth fastened onto one of her puckered nipples.

Chapter Seven

Ellie's body reacted with a pleasurable violence when Weston sucked on her nipple. She would've sworn her cry echoed around the room a few times before settling into silence once again. She'd never thought a man's mouth could make her so wanton, but Weston's had. The gooseflesh he was causing made her shiver as if the temperature in the chamber had dropped, but she knew her skin was practically on fire.

She opened her eyes just enough to see that he was now kneeling between her legs as his hands and mouth wandered over her torso.

Mercy, but it felt so good. He was so big and strong. Why hadn't she been this aware of his body before? Well, perhaps she had last night on the balcony, but now it was more real to her than ever. She'd always admired Weston's beautifully chiseled lips. She'd even found herself staring at them from time to time. Now that she knew what they were capable of, she was simply mad about them.

"Ellie," he murmured. "Your skin is so soft, like the petals of a flower. So beautiful. And your scent — " His nose tickled a trail across her chest as he inhaled, which sent more waves of gooseflesh over her skin.

"Weston," she breathed. "What is happening to me?"

He looked at her with hooded eyes from above her belly. "You're excited. Your body is telling you that you are a woman. It's giving you a woman's feelings."

"I want more," she whispered.

"Yes, my Ellie, I'll give you more."

She felt his fingers at the drawstrings of her pantalets and shivered at the thought of being at the mercy of this wicked, beautiful man that she had not truly known existed until he kissed her. He tugged her undergarments over her hips and swept them from her legs, tossing them over the side to where the cover had disappeared.

She watched with a pounding heart as he took in the sight of her, and gasped as he reached out a hand to smooth it over the curls at the juncture of her thighs.

His hands moved to her hips but she desperately wanted his hand back between her legs.

"Weston, please — "

He stared into her eyes, his gaze serious. "Ellie, if I make you come, I don't think I will be able to quell the urge to be inside you. I will try to be honorable, but you are so beautiful. If I were to lose command of my senses in the heat of the moment, I would take your maidenhead."

She swallowed, not quite understanding what it all meant, but when he mentioned her maidenhead, she took notice. This was serious. It could mean her ruin. "And no other man would want me after that?" she whispered dejectedly.

"I would kill any man who would lay a hand on you," came his fierce reply.

She stared at Weston. He was never passionate like this, at least not around her.

He swallowed and cleared his throat. "What I meant to say was that I don't think I could allow another man to have you."

She watched him, searching his eyes for an explanation to his admission. "What do you mean?"

His voice dropped to tones so low that she had to strain to hear him. "Do you want me as much as I want you?"

Ellie didn't wish to appear too eager, lest he flee. She had heard that men didn't appreciate being forced to marry a girl just because she was promiscuous with him. She drew her lower lip between her teeth, and with the barest of nods, she answered him.

Weston whispered Ellie's name and nuzzled the skin just beneath her belly button. He reached up to take of one of her hands, holding it tenderly, with his other he stroked her curls, as if getting her used to being touched.

Ellie lifted her hips and pressed into his hand. "Please," she whispered.

"Not a very patient girl, are you?" he chuckled.

She lifted her head and spoke breathlessly to him. "Weston, if you tease me now, I'll never speak to you again." She didn't really mean it, but she needed to say it nonetheless.

"You're right. I'm sorry," he said grinning. "How is this?" He parted her skin and slid his fingers up either side of her straining pearl.

Ellie's head fell back onto the pillow and she squeezed his hand, moaning his name.

He began to play with her flesh, drawing little circles, slowly at first, stroking and rubbing at her until she was practically crazed. Her throat was dry from panting, but God, he was so skilled she never wanted him to stop.

When his playing became more focused — the circles faster, tighter, she drew in a breath as the sweetest pain-pleasure held her suspended, on the verge of something grand — and it frightened her.

"Let it go, Ellie. That's it. Now come hard."

At his prompting she released her fear. Her body convulsed and trembled as waves of desire overtook her. She'd heard herself cry out, but was too drowned in the bliss of it to care about her lack of restraint. She had never achieved this beautiful height on her own.

Once her shuddering diminished, Weston stretched out next to her again and held her gently in his arms. Sheltered by his body, Ellie pressed herself to him, trying not to be embarrassed about what had just happened.

"Ellie," he whispered, his voice straining in what sounded like some sort of pain. "I am going to give you one last chance to keep your virtue intact."

She looked at Weston, her gaze incredulous. "Are you saying that I am still a virgin, even after what just happened?"

Weston grinned and pressed his head to hers. "Certainly. We didn't have intercourse."

Ellie pressed her lips together for a moment before she spoke. "Does intercourse feel as wonderful as what we just did?"

He groaned and reached for the opening of his breeches when a knock came at the door.

Both Ellie and Weston sat up and froze.

"Don't answer, Weston!" she whispered frantically.

"I must. What if it's Gwen? I have her key, and she'd bust down the door if no one responded to the call."

Ellie licked her dry lips and nodded. She took a steadying breath. "Who is there?"

A male voice answered her in Italian.

She looked at Weston, knowing her eyes were wide as saucers.

"He says he is delivering packages for Gwen," Weston interpreted.

"What shall we do?"

"*Un momento, por favore,*" Weston answered for Ellie. He ascended from the bed and tossed her the cover from the floor.

While Weston saw to the man at the door, Ellie took a moment to think as she slipped into her pantalets and tied them at her waist, then haphazardly donned her chemise. Up until Weston had entered her room, she had no idea how much he meant to her. He had always been there, watching out for her and Gwennie, ever since she could remember. He was so handsome and he had the same sense of humor Ellie did.

But what they were doing—as much as she had wanted to know about these things—was most unconventional for an unmarried man and woman. It was one thing to think about, but doing it? Their actions could be construed as wicked, and reckless, and, and… She sighed. And she'd loved every minute of it.

With her hand shaking slightly, she reached for the neckline of her chemise and tugged it so that it rested evenly upon her shoulders.

Weston placed the packages onto a settee and turned to Ellie.

"I'm sorry, Weston. We shouldn't have done this."

"I know. The blame lies with me," he murmured guiltily.

Ellie took a few steps and closed the distance between them, unsure if she was happy or disappointed that he'd agreed so readily. "No, you gave me the choice to stop, and I didn't want you to."

Weston shook his head and took her by the hands. "If I had been able to keep my hands from you and just tend to your headache, nothing further would have occurred."

They stood there in the dim light looking at each other. Ellie didn't know what should be said next in such a circumstance. Finally, she spoke. "Well, if it makes you feel any more at ease, your Chinese method of curing my head pain worked."

Weston gave her a crooked smile. "I think the Chinese would cane me for what I did to your sweet innocence, today," he said and gave her hands a squeeze.

She giggled.

"Then you are not angry with me?" he asked tentatively.

Ellie shook her head. "How could I be? I almost feel…closer to you than before," she confessed.

Weston drew her into his arms and hugged her. "Are we for exploring the city, then?"

Ellie pulled back to look into his eyes. "In a word, yes," she smiled. "And shopping, too."

He nodded. "Done. Meet me in the lobby when you're ready."

Ellie released his hands. "I'll be down soon."

Wes hobbled down the stairs to the parlor. The swelling between his legs had subsided, but the tight knot in the pit of his stomach pestered him. If the delivery man hadn't interrupted them, he would have taken Ellie's innocence.

"Good God," he murmured and dragged a hand through his hair, throwing himself into a chair. He needed to think. Hell, he needed a drink. But what he needed most was to bury his flesh into Ellie and not come up for days. Nothing could slake this need. Nothing but her.

Wes ran a hand down his face. He wasn't usually attracted to innocence. His liaisons had always been knowledgeable in the art of sexuality, and Ellie? Ellie was completely — artless. None of the women he had been with had reacted to his touch the way she had. God, he'd been so hard he could have come in his breeches like an untried lad. Ellie was ladylike and delicate. Beauty and innocence. She was everything he wasn't, and yet she was his perfect match.

Had he known it all along? He grinned and shook his head. How would he survive this trip when the very scent of her would probably make him hard?

Ellie came down the grand marble staircase, her dark hair and glowing cheeks a stunning contrast to her simple cream walking gown and straw bonnet. She looked like a delicate pastry as she walked across the lobby floor to stand before him. Wes stood.

"I'm ready now," she said, gazing directly into his eyes.

She was so brave. She could have cried off and stayed in her room all day, but here she was, offering her trust to one so unworthy. "Your beauty is ever ready, my dear, and for that I am eternally grateful." He offered her his elbow and she took it.

"Flatterer," she teased and they swept out the doors.

Chapter Eight

Gwendolyn had to refrain from purchasing everything that caught her fancy. She imagined the items she'd already sent back with the valet she'd employed from *Signore* Bernardo, took up all available space in the room.

At teatime, she sat out of doors in front of the Florian, a stylish café in Piazza San Marco. She sipped on a cup of chocolate and not tea, which made her feel continental and quite rebellious. With everyone around her masked, in fancy dress and focusing on their own revelry, no one bothered to question the fact that she lingered at the café unescorted.

Her *Moretta* mask she'd placed into her reticule that hung from her wrist, as it was not at all designed to wear during a meal. She watched as the revelers milled about the large square, laughing and interacting as if they hadn't a care in the world. *Carnevale* was a wondrous thing to behold, she thought, as she drained the last of the sweet, rich drink from her cup.

A shadow fell over her table. Gwendolyn looked up and shaded her eyes from the sun. An older man was there, holding a rose out to her and speaking Italian.

"*Scusarme, il signore, Io no parlo Italiano.*" Gwendolyn hoped she hadn't bungled the only phrase Weston had taught her to let people know that she didn't speak Italian.

The old man smiled and laid the flower across the table in front of her and walked away.

Gwendolyn took up the perennial and held the bloom, smiling as she drew in its perfume. *Who in the world would be able to produce a perfect rose in early March?* She froze. Looking around, she caught sight of a tall-cloaked figure just before he turned the corner north out of *Piazza San Marco*.

It's him!

Hastily she fumbled around in her reticule until she fished out the required coin and placed it on the table. She plunged her gloves into her bag, then took up the old man's offering. Without a second thought, she gave chase, scurrying toward the walkway the cloaked figure had taken. *Who is he? Has he been following me around Venice all day?* She narrowed her eyes and pursed her lips, focusing on the last spot she'd seen him.

Rounding the corner, Gwendolyn then quickened her steps as she watched the figure dash down the narrow walkway, his broad shoulders practically scraping the walls as he went. He cut around another corner and she followed. It almost seemed as if she was catching up when suddenly he made another right hand turn. Dashing forward, she found herself back in Piazza San Marco and scanned the area for the tall, dark figure. Out of the corner of her eye, she observed a yard of black fabric billow through the double doors of Saint Mark's Basilica— a stunning Catholic church which once was part of the Doge's palace she'd had every intention of visiting, just not in this hurried way. The doors closed, but that small deterrent didn't dissuade Gwendolyn from her quest.

Determined to get to the bottom of this mystery, she took a deep breath, steeling herself against the trembling in her stomach.

As the doors of the Basilica shut behind her, Gwendolyn's eyes took longer than she was comfortable with adjusting to the darkness. A bank of candles at the front of the church drew her toward it, as it was the brightest spot in the vast room. She moved to the side of the sanctuary as not to walk down the center aisle like a bride—a superstitious thought she admitted, but avoided doing so nonetheless.

From out of the obscurity of what she originally thought to be a small curtained doorway, a large gloved hand shot out and covered her mouth, preventing her from calling out. Another hand brusquely drew her inside, pressing her back against the solid wall of a very male chest.

"You should not follow strangers, *Signorina*," the deep Italian accent whispered close to her ear.

Recognizing the voice, Gwendolyn relaxed slightly in his grip and he removed his hand from over her mouth. "Strangers? The only thing strange about you is that I have not seen your face."

He chuckled, still holding her body against his. "Why is it that in all situations, you conduct yourself like a woman who is familiar with the streets, and yet in my arms you tremble like a little girl?"

"Nonsense. I am not trembling."

He turned her in his arms and pulled her flush against his body. "Indeed, you are."

At once, Gwendolyn felt the rigidity of his groin between them but refused to think on it. "You must be mistaken," she rebutted breathlessly. "And besides, if you were any kind of gentleman…"

The man chuckled, sending shivers over her skin that she insisted on ignoring. She continued. "Were you following me?" she asked boldly.

"Perhaps."

She could hear the smile in his voice and it perturbed her something awful. "Why?"

He drew in an annoyed breath that hissed through his teeth. "Why must you insist on knowing *everything*?" he demanded wryly, then fidgeted a bit as he removed his gloves behind her back.

"I have a right to know! And as for knowing everything, I know nothing about you." She almost commented on the fact that there was no need for him to be divesting himself of his gloves. But she knew that his answer would contain a sinister confession that she was not inclined to hear, let alone tolerate.

His amusement rumbled in his chest. God, but she hated it when he laughed at her. "You know a few things."

Gwendolyn heard the scrape of metal rings as he drew the curtain of the box they now occupied closed. If ever the dark could get darker, it just had.

"What is that supposed to−?" His arm tightened around her waist, and he began caressing the bodice of her dress.

Gwendolyn's rose fell to the floor.

"You know that I like to touch you," he purred near her ear, "and we both know you enjoy my hands upon your flesh."

"How dare you!" Gwendolyn protested, trying to squirm away from the touch that already had her civilized intentions in disagreement with her rebellious body.

"Shh. Be still and learn your second lesson."

"You arrogant bast—"

His lips came down on hers, stopping her tirade. He kissed her long and deep while with his free hand he explored her décolletage and lower.

Gwendolyn's mind spun, his masculine scent filling her lungs, her head—her equilibrium floating free. She found herself awash in awareness, not seeing but feeling everything around her. His fingers delved into the cleavage above the low, square collar of her dress, lifting her breasts until her now hard nipples were exposed to him. His fingertips thrummed over the sensitive peaks, and Gwendolyn fairly swooned at the shocking yet wickedly pleasant sensation. When had she stopped trying to break his hold? A sigh threatened to escape her throat, but she refused it venomously.

While his lips worked their way down her neck, she found her voice, as shaky as it was. "Have you no decency? We are in a church!"

He tugged her neckline lower so that it cradled her breasts. "You are Catholic?" he asked and his tongue lapped lower toward her protruding flesh, not seeming to care at all what her answer was.

"Of course not, but I at least thought you would be," she whispered, appalled that her voice sounded so frantic.

"I was." There was that damned smile in his voice again. "However, I was excommunicated long ago."

"No doubt for something as debauched as what you are doing to me now." Her sentence ended in a high-pitched squeak, and he mumbled something in Italian.

Dear God. His fingers and mouth performed on her flesh in succession. First, he would moisten her nipples with his tongue then his fingers would go to work, twisting and tugging until the dry skin necessitated another laving. Then he'd begin again as she focused and absorbed the sensations he caused. She tilted her head back. Oh how badly she wanted him to toy like this with what lay damp and throbbing between her legs. Gwendolyn closed her eyes against her shameful revelation.

"There is no greater triumph than when you surrender to me like this," he whispered.

Gwendolyn lifted her head, her vision attempting to locate some glimmer of illumination in the darkness. She took a breath to reprimand him when they both paused at the rustle of fabric and scrape of metal curtain rings in the box next to them. Through the screen, the smallest amount of light seeped in, framing the Italian rogue's thick head of hair. However, his face was still immersed in shadow.

"Do not make a sound," he breathed near her ear, and to her horror, he raised her skirt and slipped his hand into the southerly opening of her pantalets.

"*Lei e qui fare la confessione?*" an older man said from behind the screen.

"*Grazi, no Padre,*" he said with sincerity as his fingers found their goal. "*Io Sono Semplicemente in preghiera.*"

The priest left without any further comment, but hadn't fully replaced the curtain on his side of the box. A tiny amount of light remained, and Gwendolyn felt an odd combination of relief and horror—horror at the realization that she wanted whatever he was about to offer. But she'd be damned if she'd let him in on her little secret.

"Release me this instant!" She hissed her demand, though it sounded feeble to her own ears.

"Not yet, *mia dolce ciliegia*." He sank to his knees.

God, he was under her skirts, nudging her feet apart, parting the slit in her drawers. *Yes— Touch me, touch me*, her rebellious body seemed to chant. She stretched her hands out to either wall of the little room they occupied to steady herself, but was barely able to reach across the expanse. She squeezed her eyes shut and spoke to distract herself from the dizziness. "W— what does that mean, *mia dolce ciliegia*?" The phrase hadn't sounded nearly as smooth as when it came from his lips.

"My sweet cherry," he said, just before his mouth connected with the heated flesh at the juncture of her thighs.

Gwendolyn's legs nearly gave out when his hot tongue drew her tiny nub between his lips. "You mustn't—" she panted. "We shouldn't—oh God!" She squeezed her eyes shut. He was sucking on her now, holding her against his face, his hands on her bottom. She couldn't have moved away if she'd wanted to.

"So, so sweet," he murmured between her legs and lapped at her, drawing her flesh between his lips.

Gwendolyn opened her eyes at the sensation. In the dim light, she caught a faint gleam of what must have been a rod of some sort over her head. She reached up and, finding it secure, she gripped it with both hands, relieved to know that she wouldn't topple over now. Discovering that it was able to support her entire weight, she let herself hang from the bar. What a wickedly delicious feeling to be suspended while he licked at her as if she were a confection.

The waves that crashed over her were wonderfully intense, her body convulsing against his mouth while he sucked her, holding tightly to her bottom. She wanted to scream so badly, but knew her voice would echo like a banshee's in the sanctuary of the Basilica.

All of a sudden her flesh became excruciatingly sensitive. "Stop! Oh, please stop! I can't—" she whimpered, her voice hushed and ragged.

He let her go and stood, smoothing her skirts over her panniers. His hands slid from her hips up to the wrists above her head and tapped on the bar. "I shall look into acquiring one of these," he murmured, pulling her body close to his.

Still panting, Gwendolyn released her grip, appallingly embarrassed. "Please do not do so on my account," she murmured and adjusted her reticule that had slipped to her shoulder.

"On your account is precisely why I would have it installed." He took the sides of her face as if he were going to kiss her again.

Without pausing to think about it, Gwendolyn bravely placed her hands on the sides of his face.

He froze.

Her hands slid up to his fevered forehead then to his sharp, high cheekbones. She traced the hollows of his cheeks and finally, smoothed her fingers across his hard, square jaw, stopping as she felt the cleft at his chin. *He must be beautiful.*

Suddenly he seized her wrists. "No," he said simply, not threateningly, not with anger, not even a command.

"Why?"

"I won't have you dragged into my problems. It would be better if you could not be forced to point me out in a crowd."

"Wha—?"

"By the time you leave for home, *Signorina* Rawleigh, you will be able to walk away without incident."

Gwendolyn gritted her teeth. "And what do you call this, what we just did? I would say that having your hands and mouth on my body is quite a *critical* incident, sir."

He took hold of her upper arms. "You don't understand. It is dangerous to know me."

"That is the most ridiculous thing I have ever heard," she spat her words at him, tired of his game. "Keep your identity, you rake, and more to the point, keep your hands to yourself!" Gwendolyn turned on her heel, threw back the long velvet curtain, and stormed out of the church without looking back.

Marcello watched her depart. When the doors to the Basilica shut behind her, he swore, his voice sounding hollow inside the confessional box. *Signorina* Gwendolyn Rawleigh was irresistible to him, and she hated the very air he breathed.

His rebellious body strained against his breeches, crying out for release. Marcello had to get out of the church without being seen. He only had a hooded cloak to hide him from the ones who sought him. He'd forgotten to don a mask before he left the *palazzo* this morning, a mistake which would not be repeated, not after today.

He certainly hadn't planned on Gwendolyn chasing him until he was caught. He grinned in the darkness. *Perhaps I wanted to be caught by her, damn it.* She acted so haughty in public, as if she fully understood what he wanted from her, what any functioning man with a brain and its corresponding organs would want from her. When he'd made a move to take it from her, she'd melted into a shivering puddle, then became a boiling cauldron once she'd become acquainted with his touch.

What man in his prime could resist producing such a transformation?

* * * *

Ellie could not bring herself to depart from Weston's company, even to change for dinner. They sat in the parlor at an adorable matching table and chairs set next to a window, the magnetism between them palpable.

They had wandered in and out of shops for the better part of the day, admiring the enduring Venetian architecture and just enjoying each other's companionship. She took pleasure in watching him converse with the locals. He spoke Italian wonderfully, and the people seemed to like him very much. The dear fellow didn't once complain, even when she's spent extra time at the perfumery, searching for just the right item.

She watched him now as his graceful, long fingers delicately held the stem of his wineglass. Being so intimately familiar with his hands she knew, were he inclined to do so, his strong digits could snap the thin glass in two. A shiver ran over her skin at the thought.

She felt heat creep up her cheeks under his steady gaze. He sipped his wine, watching her over the rim of the glass, his eyes never leaving hers. She couldn't remember seeing him in any other light than that of the man he turned out to be. It was as if he were a different person altogether, yet familiar.

Sitting forward, Weston took a deep breath, as if what he was about to say was of great import. "I was thinking, just now. How you would feel if, say…"

Ellie leaned toward him when he paused. "Go on."

Wes watched as Ellie's delicate eyebrows rose in question over her big blue eyes. He drained his glass and set it down. "Do you suppose we might…? That is to say, would you be inclined to…?" He blinked. *Damnation.* If he stopped now, he'd not be able to screw up the courage to ask her again. He had to forge ahead. She had been so agreeable with him over the past few hours while they strolled about Venice and stopped for a quick bite at a quaint little cafe. He swallowed. He had to ask, or he'd regret if for the rest of his life. "Do you think we could…?" He glanced down at the table and back up to Ellie and swallowed. "Be alone again?"

Chapter Nine

Ellie's eyes went wide at first, then her face flushed prettily just before her gaze became as hot as her cheeks. From where he sat, Wes could feel the heat radiating from her person, from her searing stare, and all he'd done was suggest they take up where they'd left off. *God, but she is an enchanting beauty.* His cock twitched in full agreement. He felt more than saw her décolletage rise while she took a breath to speak.

At that very delicate, crucial moment, Gwendolyn decided to make an appearance.

"Oh, what a day! Ellie, Weston," Gwendolyn nodded her greeting. "I hope the party tonight is not too far away. I'm quite famished."

He knew Ellie daren't respond to his query now.

Ellie sat back in her chair and smiled pleasantly. "Ah, Gwennie. What time does the soirée start?"

"Eight, I believe." Gwendolyn looked over her shoulder at a tall, stunning ornate clock that stood against a wall. "Oh good heavens! It's nearly six! Come, Ellie. We must get ready."

Gwendolyn turned on her heel, but somehow must have sensed that Ellie had not made a move to stand. She turned back to her friend and her brother. "Ellie? What are you waiting for?"

"N-nothing." Ellie stood, took up her purchase from the table, and curtsied to Weston. "What a vigorous conversation we were having, sir. I hope to continue it *very* soon," she looked him in the eyes, her blue gaze penetrating his, then turned to depart for their rooms above stairs with Gwendolyn.

Wes could do nothing but watch her retreat, his breeches far too tight for comfort. He didn't know what to do.

Ellie wanted to be alone with him again.

He wanted to shout or jump up and down or something to release some of his enthusiasm. He knew without a doubt the wait would be excruciating.

Ellie's hand shook as she reached for the marble balustrade, the flesh between her legs heating, becoming a tiny ball of exquisite pressure at the thought of being alone with Weston again. Following Gwendolyn, she turned on the landing to ascend the second set of stairs that led to the rooms. She dared not look back at Weston, for she already felt his eyes on her.

Goodness how she needed to be touched right at this very moment—needed Weston to manipulate her and wiggle her between the legs so that she would, how had he put it? Come. Yes, that was it. What an appropriate word. It was an end, and yet one could visit any time one wished.

She wondered at the fact that, when she touched herself, she felt terribly naughty, depraved even. But with Weston... With Weston it felt glorious to have his hands upon her, his lips on hers. It was if the moon, the sun and the stars all agreed that she and Weston should be together, caressing each other. *Loving* each other.

Ellie's heart pounded, and she was sure Gwendolyn could hear it from where she walked a mere two steps ahead of her.

How on earth would she get through the next three or four hours, with this insistent craving for physical pleasure she knew Weston would give her when they once again found themselves in private?

* * * *

The instant the buttons on the front of his breeches didn't seem as though they were about to pop off and shoot someone across the room in the eye, Wes acknowledged the fact that he, too, should dress for dinner. He was still hard, but he was certain it wasn't as blatant as it had been a few minutes ago. He made to push back his chair and head up to his room when Albert approached the table.

"I'm so glad I found you, Wes. I need some advice."

Wes' head was in such a fog he stared at his friend as if he were speaking a foreign language — one with which he was not familiar.

"Hello, Albert. What was that?"

"Can I get you a drink? You look rather scattered."

Wes glanced down at his empty wine glass and nodded. "My thanks."

Albert crossed the parlor to the sideboard.

One thing advantageous about Albert's arrival, Wes' breeches seemed to settle down further and fit properly once again.

Albert returned with two glasses of vermouth and sat down across from Wes. "How is Venice treating you?" He took a sip of his drink.

"Tolerably well." *I will be making love to Ellie as soon as I can get her alone.* Luckily, the comment hadn't gone any further than the back of his mind. "And you?" Wes took a swallow of his beverage.

"Very well. In fact, I have wanted to mention a potentially gainful pecuniary situation to you, but have been reluctant to do so until now."

"Really?" Wes' attention was fully on Albert. "Is that why you've been pacing like a caged tiger?"

Albert nodded once in certainty. "Indeed it is. In fact, if you are able to help in any way, I'd be glad to cut you in on the reward."

"Reward, you say? Do tell, sir. I'm always interested in lucrative monetary matters." Wes grinned. He leaned forward, placed his elbows on the table, and lifted his drink to his lips.

From Albert's seated position, he drew closer to Wes and spoke quietly. "During the crossing from England, I met two men from Florence, Italy, who said that they're looking for a man who could potentially make a claim for the Medici fortune."

"My word. That's quite a feat to be able to do such a thing. Is this man a relation to the Medicis?" He took a sip then folded his upper lip in to draw off the foam.

"Yes and no. He is the great grandson of Paolo Rise-Verdante, who was the son of Anna Maria Luisa de Medici. Apparently, his father was the result of a secret love affair between Marcello's grandmother and Giacomo IV Rise-Verdante."

"You don't say?" Wes commented then enjoyed a sip.

"The rogue's name is Marcello Verdante." Albert sampled his libation. "The men I met on the voyage over — in addition to a larger Florentine faction — had chased Verdante out of Florence, threatening to kill him if he ever returned. But apparently, he has not gone far enough away for their comfort. It has been said that he is here in Venice hiding, an easy thing to do during *Carnevale*, if you ask me."

"Hm. Is he dangerous?"

"They didn't really say as much, but it was indicated that they had quite a time of ousting him from Florence."

"So, did he try to make a claim to the fortune?"

Albert thought for a moment. "Again, not every detail was revealed to me. All I know is that they have offered a very handsome reward, and only for successfully giving them his location."

"Hm. So you are not in any danger in your quest? Well, sounds like a good, solid way to earn some extra funds."

"Yes, it does. I am very lucky they sought me out. I've been combing the city for Marcello Verdante all day long."

Weston again partook of his refreshment. "Any leads?"

Albert took three long drinks, emptying his glass altogether. "Not as of yet."

"Well, what does this Marcello Verdante look like?"

Albert shrugged a shoulder. "Tall, dark. Your regular Italian, I would suppose."

"Is that all you have to go on?"

"Well, it is said that he is wealthy in his own right, investments in a shipping company out of America — Bentley shipping or some such — a block of business real estate in London, interests in India, etcetera, but all that is neither here nor there. I understand the first thing the Florentines did before chasing him out of town, was give him a settlement of some vast amount. Unfortunately, he didn't bother to leave town fast enough, In addition," Albert scoffed, "he apparently has two men to do his dirty work for him."

"And were you given a description of them?"

"Your average Italian thugs, most like."

Out of nowhere, a vision of Ellie's porcelain flesh flashed through Wes's mind. "Well, Albert, it seems like you have some work ahead of you," he said, and tossed back the rest of his drink.

"Are you saying you are not interested in the scheme?" Albert asked, his eyes wide.

Wes grinned. "My holiday comes first, Albert. Villains come last." Weston stood and thanked him for the spirits. "I need to change for tonight's party. Will you be joining us?"

"Albert nodded. "I will. I have to keep my eyes open for Verdante, you know."

* * * *

Ellie could hardly concentrate on anything but the fact that Weston wanted to be alone with her. She smiled and made light conversation with her best friend while they dressed for the evening, regardless. The maid couldn't speak English, so she felt not at all uncomfortable with her there. "Gwennie, you are so naughty for telling our mothers we had a companion with us when you know perfectly well we didn't."

Gwendolyn grinned as she sat in the chair while the maid fashioned her powdered wig just so. "Being naughty can be fun, dear. You should try it sometime."

Ellie nearly choked. *If Gwendolyn only knew…* "You are so bad, Gwennie."

"Perhaps." There was a definite pause in Gwendolyn's speech, but in no time at all, she continued. "Besides, I knew Weston would be happy to be our guardian on this trip."

Ellie coughed to hide her mortification. She hoped Gwendolyn never found out what she and Weston had done.

Ellie felt Gwendolyn's gaze upon her person and turned fully to her.

"Ellie, I think tonight we'll find you some handsome man to—"

Ellie inhaled sharply, interrupting Gwendolyn's suggestion.

Gwendolyn stood, dismissed the maid and walked over to Ellie. She took her by the shoulders. "El, if we are to have a good time on this trip, you are going to have to loosen the strings of your societal corset. It's the whole reason we came, remember?"

At Ellie's reluctant nod, her best friend released her shoulders. Little did Gwendolyn know that Ellie's corset strings could do nothing to protect her from her own thoughts.

With burning cheeks, Ellie turned away from Gwendolyn. Thoughts of the clandestine episode with Weston caused a delightful wetness between her legs, making her feel terribly out of breath. And now she understood the mystery of it all. Weston had shown her what happens when one knew how to touch a woman's body. Ellie nearly swooned at her memories.

And the best part of it was that her handsome friend-turned lover, Weston, wanted to do it again. Lord, what she wouldn't do to scurry over to his room right now and have him put his hands and lips on her again. Her nipples hardened at the idea.

Ellie glanced over her shoulder at Gwendolyn, who was busy changing her mind yet again about her shoes for this evening's festivities. Before her encounter with Weston, Ellie had often felt guilty that she was unable to voice her thoughts and dreams to her very best friend, but every time she wanted to reveal her secret, she changed her mind in fear of seeming a degenerate.

Ellie admired Gwennie's poise and insight into womanhood. She was so at ease with the world, and Ellie felt the complete opposite. She was sure Gwendolyn would help her if she would only ask. Mercy, Gwennie was already trying to be of assistance though, wasn't she?

"Ellie, come help me with these shoes, I can't seem to make a solid decision about which ones to wear."

"Be there in a moment, Gwennie." Maybe, just maybe Ellie could get Gwendolyn to bring up the subject again, and this time she could facilitate a confession of her wicked introspections.

Chapter Ten

Later that evening, Gwendolyn smiled to herself during the dessert course, feeling as safe as if she were at home. Her powdered wig was ideal for hiding under. Not only was it a perfect fit, but she blended in with the other revelers who'd donned wigs and masks for the gala.

Her own brother had to glance at her a second time when she and Ellie emerged from their room.

"That gown is cut indecently low," Weston had commented with a frown. "Be sure not to sneeze or you will spill yourself out of it."

Rolling her gaze across the high gilt ceiling of the parlor, Gwendolyn harrumphed at Weston. "There's that motherly tone again," she said drolly but half-kidding and swept past him.

Gwendolyn was also very pleased to be out of Piazza San Marco for the evening. They'd had to take a hired rowboat across the Canale di San Marcoto Giudecca, which was part of a serpentine set of islands to the south with a bit more elbow room than where they had been staying in San Marco. The buildings and houses were not as bunched together in Giudecca, and that made room for moonlit pathways that wove in and out of lovely gardens. As soon as the dancing commenced, she would slip away to go exploring and not be missed.

Without moving her head too much, Gwendolyn shifted her eyes and scanned the room for a tall figure in black. Happily, there wasn't a single gentleman taller than her own brother, who sat speaking in quiet tones to the ever-stoic Albert.

Well, at least Albert hadn't engaged her in conversation on this trip. He'd most likely bring up that dreadful episode last year. She hoped he was at least smart enough to keep to himself for the rest of their holiday.

Dismissing Albert from her mind, Gwendolyn relaxed and sipped her sweet wine while watching the musicians file out of their little corner in the dining room. She smiled, knowing their exit to set up in the ballroom took her closer to the gardens and a taste of freedom — that is, once she had Ellie dancing with a promising partner.

Gwendolyn glanced at Ellie, who seemed as if she were in a different place all together. "El, are you well, dear? You don't seem yourself tonight."

Ellie sat up from her reclined position against the back of the chair, her gaze snapping to Gwendolyn. "I-I must have a headache or some such."

"Some such? Don't you know the root of your own irritation?"

Ellie glanced at Weston first, then Albert. "Er, yes, it is my head."

Gwendolyn expected a bit more information, but when none came she nodded. "Very well." She pushed aside her disappointment that her best friend's night had ended so soon. "Weston, would you be willing to accompany Ellie back to the hotel? She's such a delicate flower, you know."

He glanced at the girls then at Albert. "Perhaps Al—"

Gwendolyn interrupted her brother. Whatever reason he had for offering up Albert for the task, she still could not bring herself to have confidence in Weston's companion. "No, I would prefer you to be the one."

Albert scowled at Gwendolyn. "Gwendolyn, am I some sort of villain not to be trusted with your friend?"

She started thinking that perhaps Albert had read the look in her eyes if not her thoughts. "I never said—"

"Gwendolyn, I know you hold no keenness for me—"

"It isn't that," she said in a huff and crossed her arms over her chest.

"You are quite correct. I have *never* measured up to your standards."

"Albert, please," she hissed.

"Enough," Weston barked, startling Ellie, to whom he was immediately contrite. "Can you two at least be civil to one another while we are on holiday?"

Albert stood, his chair shoving back out of his way. "It seems that as long as I keep to myself, *Miss Rawleigh* is content."

Gwendolyn sighed. "Now, Albert—"

He interrupted her again and spoke directly to Weston. . "I will do my duty as your friend, Pres. When your sister leaves the party, I will be right behind her."

All three of them watched Albert storm away.

"Gwen, sometimes you can be so disagreeable," Weston admonished.

"Do stop needling. You heard your friend. He will escort me back to the palazzo when I'm ready to return. Now go take Ellie back to the room. I'll be along later."

"Gwendolyn," Weston said in a near threatening tone. "I want you to promise me that you will be gracious to Albert when he escorts you home."

"Of course I will. But if he brings up last season—"

"I will give you my very own guarantee that Albert is just as happy to put that debacle behind him as you are."

She eyed him and smiled pleasantly. "My apologies, it was difficult to read his mind once I got past his pleasing demeanor."

Weston released his frustration in a huff and stood. Gwendolyn ignored him, but watched him with a weariness in her heart. He went around to Ellie and offered her his elbow. "I should have known better than to try and put an idea into Gwen's head that she hadn't already thought of herself," he mumbled, then nodded frostily to his sister, he guided Ellie away from the table and out of the room.

* * * *

Weston's attempts at making Ellie comfortable warmed her heart. They both had removed their masks when Weston hailed a gondola. He'd fluffed the cushions before she'd taken her seat and even covered her with his cloak. He settled down next to her after informing the gondolier of their destination. Ellie watched Weston stare off into the water as they shoved off from the jetty, his face turned toward the moonlit canal. She had been eternally grateful that after the bickering came to an end, it was Weston who was to take her back to the hotel and not Albert.

"Weston?" she called to him quietly.

His gaze snapped to hers. "Is something wrong? Does your head hurt overmuch?"

Ellie smiled and glanced down at the floor of the boat. "My head seems to have made a miraculous recovery." She chuckled nervously. She wanted to look up at him so badly, but she just couldn't bring herself to do it.

Weston was quiet for some moments. When she could stand his silence no longer, she stole a quick glance at him. His face was difficult to read, but she felt the intensity of his gaze.

He finally spoke, his voice soft, quiet and with a hint of a smile mixing with his tone. "Ellie, you sly little thing. You fabricated that headache, didn't you?"

Her gaze returned to his handsome face and her growing happiness matched the subtle mirth in Weston's voice. She nodded. "You do not think ill of me for doing so, do you?"

Deftly, Weston lifted the edge of the cloak and slid in next to her. "Not at all. In fact, you surprise me, and pleasantly so."

His body felt wonderfully warm and so big and commanding next to hers, she thought she'd swoon. "Oh, I do hope that's true. I would be quite disappointed if you thought me too forward." Ellie pithily contemplated that she may have been babbling in her nervousness.

Weston smiled, his face inching closer to hers. "Ellie?"

She swallowed. "Yes?"

"I give you full rein to be as forward with me as you wish, and I promise never to fault you for it."

Ellie briefly chewed on her lower lip before replying. "Would you be shocked if I granted you that same permission?" she whispered. His face was so near now it appeared out of focus.

His answer was a bold chuckle just before he pulled her against his body, his lips claiming hers with fervor.

Chapter Eleven

Gwendolyn giggled behind gloved fingertips as she pressed herself against a garden wall. She'd slipped out the back way of the party after donning her mask, and not a single soul had noticed—not even the stoic Albert.

The moon had only just begun its waning phase, but it provided ample light for her exploration, when it wasn't hidden behind the thick, random clouds which whisked by periodically. Her charcoal gray cloak would do very well if she had to slink into the shadows, but as it turned out—much to her delight—she seemed to be the only one about this late in the evening.

Heading down a cobblestone pathway, she wound through a small grove of trees and around a lovely white stone fountain that bubbled happily at her as she passed. She eventually came to a garden with life-size statuary and a large cage with a multitude of birds asleep within. Not knowing how the birds would react were she to awaken them abruptly, she tiptoed beyond them and let herself through a darling, little garden gate. Finding yet another pathway, she followed it for a while until it ended at the edge of the islet. After finding and taking another quaint walkway then climbing a half-flight of steps, Gwendolyn found herself upon an old stone bridge, on the southern-most side of the islands, looking out over the Laguna Veneta.

The water sparkled like diamonds in the moonlight and Gwendolyn sighed at the view.

A crackle, like the sound of coarse sand beneath a well-shod foot caused Gwendolyn to freeze and hold her breath. Surely she was the only one out at this time of night. It was in Piazza San Marco that the revelers were drawn, not this sleepy little isle. She listened for a few moments and when no other noise could be heard over her own beating heart and the gentle sloshing of the water below, she continued over the bridge to the other side.

More aware of her surroundings than before, she slipped through a squeaky iron gate and took a path that led around a corner. Suddenly, she found herself in the center of a lovely wooded garden surrounded by three very high walls. She turned back and tracked the path to the entrance of the garden, but stopped short as a tall, cloaked figure occupied her escape route. Her breath caught in her throat.

The white *Bauta* mask and silk lace cravat glowed brightly in the moonlight in contrast to the menacing black of the rest of the outfit. What unnerved her further was the expanse of his shoulders brushing the gate and its latch on the opposite side.

* * * *

He and Ellie had done nothing but kiss on the way back to the Danieli, Wes doing his best not to get overly excited in case Ellie changed her mind. His efforts were futile, though, no matter how good his intentions aspired to be. His desire for her was like an all-consuming firestorm.

When they emerged from the gondola, Ellie's swollen red lips framed her crooked grin, their masks dangling daintily from her gloved fingers. Wes gave the man his coin and escorted Ellie toward the palazzo, pausing just before the door.

"Ellie, you know what will happen if I take you up to your room, don't you?"

Ellie looked at him with shining eyes and nodded.

"All you have to do is say the word, and I will allow you to go up without me."

"No. I-I want this."

He tore his gaze away and starred out into the lagoon for the briefest of moments. "I shouldn't, Ellie... I have no right—"

"Oh, please, *please* don't change your mind. Not now!"

Wes' self-control shattered at the sound of Ellie's pleading. He nearly groaned, surrendering to not only her, but to the demands of his own body. He took her by the hand and led her straight through the parlor and up the marble stairs.

At the door to her room, Ellie fumbled with the bulky key. Wes laid his hand upon hers to steady her shaking, and together they unlocked the door.

She went directly to the window after tossing her reticule and the masks in a chair, and threw open the curtains, letting in the moonlight that occasionally peeked out from between the clouds.

Wes came up behind her and slipped his arms around her waist. He moved her brunette ringlets aside with his nose and kissed the spot between her shoulder and neck. "God, you smell good." He thought he'd heard her giggle.

She turned in his arms, her gaze directed at his lips. "Kiss me again."

Her words were somewhere between a sweet demand and a shy question. He grinned down at her, disregarding his pounding heart. "How could I refuse such a comely maiden?" He cupped her cheeks with gentle urgency and lowered his mouth to hers.

There was no doubt in his mind that she had the most wonderful lips he'd ever kissed. He stilled as she reached up on her tiptoes, steadying herself with his shoulders. She experimented with him, sampling him—first his bottom lip, then his top. She made a sweet little noise in the back of her throat, then shyly nudged his mouth open and slid her tongue inside.

Wes could no longer stand it. His blood hummed in his ears and coursed through his body. The temperature of his skin rose to a fever. He slid his hands down her back, tightened his arms around her waist and entwined his tongue with hers. After a few moments, the kiss became wild, their breathing ragged as each tasted the other's need.

Ellie ended the kiss and whispered, "Help me out of my gown."

His jaw locked tight against the intensity of his erection, her soft voice doing nothing to alleviate the feeling. Dizzy with desire and the promise of what was to come, he turned her by the waist so her back faced him. Deftly he began unlacing, untying, unhooking and divesting her of the fine fabric that separated them. She stepped out of the forgotten garments wearing only the least of her underpinnings and turned to face her eager lover.

* * * *

Gwendolyn's already irregular breath stuttered as the intruder murmured something in Italian.

"Er, excuse me, I need to pass through that gate," she indicated the space behind the figure who blocked her path.

"You should not have wandered so far from the *ballo, Signorina.*"

Gwendolyn swallowed. The mask he wore made it difficult to ascertain whether or not it was that same rake whose path she'd been repeatedly crossing. His accent solid, as was the deep tone of his voice, but the sound rang different—hollow, otherworldly.

Her mind rushed for a topic that would cover her rapidly unraveling nerves. "I would have your name, *Signore*. I am Miss Rawleigh."

He chuckled and crossed his ample arms over his thick chest. "No matter how much you wish to know my name, the answer is still the same."

It *was* him again. His tone sounded sarcastic, mocking even, which didn't serve to endear him to her any further than what had already been established. Gwendolyn relaxed a bit, but other, more hair-raising notions made their presence known in her mind.

"Why did you follow me?"

"So that you would remain safe," he murmured and leaned casually against the wall.

"Safe? When am I ever safe with you?" She stomped a slippered foot on the path to drive her point home.

"Believe me, *mia ciliegia*, there are many men who would have taken that which you hold most dear at your first encounter with them."

Gooseflesh rolled over her body at the sound of his pet name for her, and she both hated it and loved it at the same time. "Do not call me... How would you know what I hold most dear?" Gwendolyn was embarrassed at how her agitation caused her sentences to run into each other.

He pushed away from the wall and began moving toward her. "Have you forgotten so soon, then?"

"Forgotten? Forgotten what?" she asked, her voice beginning to escalate, her steps retreating from his advance.

"Perhaps we need to revisit your second lesson."

Damn if she couldn't hear the smile in his voice, even though the shape of the mask made him sound unearthly. Her heart began to pound as she remembered for the thousandth time, what his skilled hands and lips were capable of doing to her.

"No! I mean, I remember. I remember with perfect clarity." Gwendolyn held out her hands as if that would stop his advance.

He reached out and took her by the upper arms. His grip did not hurt by any means, but it was insistent and demanding in a very sensual way. Oh how she cursed her betraying body and mind for thinking so. At once, her back met a cool brick wall.

"Then tell me. Tell me what you remember."

"I cannot say."

"I think you can."

"No."

"Yes," he coaxed. He released her arm and began drawing her skirts up. "Or we shall revisit the lesson here and now."

She felt the drag of his fingers up the front of her thigh and gasped. "I remember—y-your lips."

"What about my lips?"

"I remember them on…on my…"

"On your what?" he asked and with his knee, nudged her thighs apart.

"On my body," she ended feebly. Underneath her mask she felt the heat of her cheeks as if they were on fire.

"What else do you remember? There must be more." He stroked the back of his hand down the front of her drawers.

Gwendolyn's breath became labored. "Your tongue."

"Yes, go on," he urged as he strummed his knuckles over her womanhood.

"I remember your tongue, how it teased me." She gasped when he pressed his hand between her legs through the thin cotton fabric. "Your mouth, how it suckled me, and I remember dying at the sensation." She breathed her words out in a sigh, her forehead falling forward onto the lacy folds of his silk-clad chest.

Much to her mortification, Gwendolyn began to weep.

Chapter Twelve

Marcello froze. He had not meant to cause Gwendolyn pain, physical or otherwise. He tossed her skirts back over her panniers and brought her body forward, wrapping his arms around the small of her back. "Why do you cry? Have I hurt you?"

She shook her head and sniffled, but instead of words, another sob escaped her lips.

Despite his raging erection, Marcello felt like a cad. He had no business with this girl, and yet, here he was, practically assaulting her. He grimaced. Yes, that had been a harsh thought, but he had to remind himself that he was in no position to coax Miss Rawleigh to his bed, let alone allow her to sample certain pleasures that only a sexually skilled woman should be privy to. Promoting himself to be her educator was not truly his job. A proper husband should be the one to give her her first kiss, her first orgasm, her first — everything.

But damn it, she was irresistible.

She sniffed again and raised her head to speak. "I am crying because I am such a wanton."

"You are not a wanton."

"I am so," she argued, her breath catching in her throat involuntarily. "I wanted to know what a man's lips felt like. I've wanted to know for some time now." She sniffed delicately. "And when you put them on my body, on a place that I would never have dreamt of, all I can think about is — *that*." She sniffed again and gestured to nothing in particular, but he knew to what she was referring. "And on top of all of this immoral behavior, I let you do these things to me, and I don't even know who you are!" she sobbed. "I may as well be asking for money!"

"Oh, *mia dolce*." He hugged her tightly to console her bruised ego. "You are not that type of woman. You are sweet and charming."

"No, I'm used and — and wicked." She sobbed even harder.

Marcello would have laughed, but he knew it would offend her delicate emotional state. He lifted her away from his chest and tilted her chin up with a knuckle. "You are the woman of every man's dreams," he whispered.

A harsh sound erupted from her throat that he thought may have been an attempt at laughter. "Oh, indeed. A woman of the streets, more like"

He shook his head. "No. You would make the perfect wife."

She made the sound again. "You lie, sir."

"Listen to me." With the tips of his fingers he gave her chin a soft shake. "You are polite and demure in public."

"Polite? I'm a flirt!" The corners of her generous lips curved toward the ground and she tilted her head forward.

He caught her before she began crying again. "There is nothing wrong with a little flirting, as long as you stop before things get out of hand."

"And I don't know when to stop, apparently," she murmured dejectedly.

"You do now. May I be so bold as to say that you were very lucky to have found your wings with me?"

Gwendolyn sighed, her breath heaving in and out of her lungs. "Don't you see? I *deserve* the label of wanton. You are a stranger. You won't even tell me your name."

"I've told you, my situation is not very friendly at the moment. This has *nothing* to do with you."

She went on as if she had not heard him. "Would I have been sitting like a proper lady in the first place, you would never have noticed me."

"No, you are quite wrong." Honestly, there wasn't a shred of truth to her statement. He had noticed her the very moment she'd entered the dining room the night of the first ball. He was fascinated with her. From an alcove hidden by a large potted fern he'd watched her conquer the entire male population of the room. Yes, she'd painted the picture of a woman who knew her way around the bedroom, but that was only secondary. The regal way in which she held herself, her steps as she floated across the floor, her impeccable manners as she enjoyed the meal, her deep honey colored hair he longed to comb his fingers through. Just as he took a breath to tell her, the gate to the garden swung open on its rusty hinges.

Marcello froze. If his enemies walked through that gate, he was done for. There was nowhere to run, nor was there a proper weapon within reach with which to defend himself or Gwendolyn. He glanced down at the beautiful woman in front of him. *Dios*! How could he have let himself forget the fact that he was in continual danger?

Placing his index finger over Gwendolyn's lips, Marcello wordlessly asked for her silence.

* * * *

Ellie gazed at Weston from where she stood in the beam of moonlight, in her corset, pantalets and stockings. He was so handsome she could have cried.

"Ellie," Weston breathed and stepped toward her, taking her in his arms.

She grinned and began removing the pins from her hair. When the last pin was out and her curls tickled her shoulders and upper arms, Weston pulled her to him.

"You are torturing me, El," he said then plunged his fingers into her hair. With his hands, he gently embraced her head then slid down to rub the muscles of her neck.

Weston kissed crisscross paths over her face down to her chest, and she wanted so badly for him to be able to reach everywhere he could. She began tugging the corset strings at her back, but they knotted.

"Here, allow me." He slid his hands to her waist and squeezed. For an instant, his surprising strength took her breath away. The busk of her corset buckled and he separated the hooks and eyes at the front of her stays faster than she could have done it herself. Ellie nearly swooned at the power he'd displayed. At every turn, he was manlier than the moment before, and it thrilled her by leaps and bounds.

The garment fell to the floor, her lungs expanded as she was no longer at the confining mercy of the corset, the air felt cool against her skin.

His hands immediately gravitated to her breasts, and Ellie's knees turned to porridge. Weston caught her up and carried her to the bed.

"Aren't you going to take your clothes off?" Shocking herself with her own words she pressed her lips together.

He held her in his arms and grinned. "Why, Eleanor Madeline Appleton," he teased.

She giggled at the use of her full name as he placed her upon the blankets. Ellie rolled over and hid her face in the pillow. She had no idea he knew her middle name.

It wasn't long until she felt the mattress dip as he lay down next to her.

"Are you playing hide and seek, my lady?" he asked, brushing his fingertips across her back.

Ellie shivered a little. "In a word, yes," she replied loud enough so that her muffled voice would reach him. He chuckled and settled his body over her back. He felt light, so he must have been holding most of his muscled weight from her. Lord, but he was warm. She lifted and wiggled her bum a little to let him know she knew what he was doing.

"Ellie," he murmured as she felt him press down upon her bottom.

She was suddenly aware of something poking between her legs, nudging at her as if asking permission before invading. Her heart increased its tempo. She was sure there was no greater feeling in the world than that of her lover's strength surrounding her, warming her, and maybe even demanding that she do what he wanted. Mercy, but she was breathless with the thought. Ellie was prepared to surrender to him, to have him take her body and pleasure it until she cried out. She'd wanted this from Weston all day long, and now here they were, willing to give each other everything. She grinned to herself. Her head turned to the side and she opened her eyes. "I can feel you," she murmured and lifted her bottom again for emphasis.

He groaned. "Turn over."

He lifted himself while she rolled onto her back, and he settled next to her. She reached for him. "May I touch you, too?" she asked quietly.

She could see his slight grin in the dimness of the room. "How you surprise me. Of course you may."

She rolled onto her hip and took hold of him. A moan escaped from deep within his throat. His strong male body was completely foreign to her, this part in particular. It was big and hard, yet soft—its tip not quite as rigid as the shaft. She wished there was more light in the room so that she could see what she was feeling. She listened to his breathing and wondered how much longer he would allow her exploration.

"What feels best?" she asked, her voice trembled slightly, but she didn't care.

"What do you mean?"

"What feels best, if I touch you this way—?" She held him in one hand, petting him like a kitten. "Or this way—?" She cradled the tip of him in the palm of her hand.

"Everything. All of it. Your hands feel wonderful, no matter how you touch me," he replied just above a whisper and placed a few kisses across her forehead.

"Everything? There must be a very best way. Tell me. Show me. I want to know how you like it."

He got on all fours over Ellie, his legs spread, his manly bits dangling over the juncture of her thighs. She was so excited she could hardly stand it. *He's going to do it. He's going to take me.* She reached up and briefly pressed the back of her fingers to her burning cheek. Her breasts jiggled with every shift of the mattress under them and she relished the intimacy of it all.

"Now, hold onto me here." He maneuvered her free hand so that her fingers were circling his shaft.

"Am I doing it right? I can't seem to get my hand all the way around it."

She thought she heard him begin to laugh but it was more like a breath. "That will do. Now, take your other hand and reach below."

Her hand was now resting on the sack underneath, but it was higher and tighter than any statuary she had admired before. She explored the new piece with curious fingers, feeling the soft hairs and somewhat pliable flesh. Ellie wanted to press her lips and body to it, to feel the springy hairs rubbing against her nipples. At once, she noticed that Weston was trembling.

"Is this right?" she asked.

"Oh, *so* right," he murmured. "I want you to stroke up and down like this." He covered her hand with his and gently slid her touch up almost to the tip and down, very near the hilt. "God, Ellie. That's it, right there."

She grinned and fondled him with fluttering fingers. "So you do like to be petted like a kitten."

At once, he placed his hand over hers. "Stop! You must stop now."

Ellie extracted her hands. "Did I do something wrong?"

Weston collapsed next to her on the bed. "No, no. I'm not ready to spend myself quite yet."

"But I want to—" Ellie's breath caught in her throat as Weston tugged the strings at the top of her pantalets. With her help, he slid them from her body and removed her stockings. She lay before him as naked as the day she was born, and the excited gooseflesh prickled her from her ankles to her scalp. Oh, if he would only hurry and begin touching her!

"I'll make you a promise, Ellie."

"Yes?" she whispered breathlessly.

"If you want to take me all the way to completion with only your hands, you can, but some other time. Right now I want to give you pleasure."

He grinned as Ellie nodded frantically. He was going to touch her now and she shivered in her excitement.

"Good girl," he said and slid his hand between her thighs.

Chapter Thirteen

"Scusarci, il Signore, la Signorina."

He turned away from Gwendolyn and she could now see that there were two men standing on the pathway.

"May we see some identification?" one of them asked in heavily Italian accented English, then repeated the question in Italian.

From out of her companion's mouth came something she would never thought to have heard.

"Good God, man! We're on our honeymoon!"

He had spoken with an accurate aristocratic British accent. It reminded her of the times she had listened through the keyhole to her father's study while he'd chatted with friends. Something in the back of her mind caused her to think that perhaps he did this to keep his identity a secret. So she chimed in with the only accent she knew how to do well.

"Och, can ye Venetians myend yer oon business?"

The two men put their heads together for a few moments and came up apologizing in Italian and

English. They bowed and scurried away. The gate closed behind them.

Gwendolyn covered her laughter with a gloved hand, but lost her mirth as he took her by the wrist and hauled her toward the gate. "We must leave this place."

"Now?"

"Yes, as soon as those thugs are out of sight. I will take you back to the ball and you can do what you wish. But I must retire for the evening."

Quicker than she could respond, he pulled her through the gate and onto a path she had not taken before. She was twisted around as the moon was now behind the clouds. They walked hurriedly for some time, her companion looking over his shoulder what seemed like every few steps.

At once she heard his breath catch and instantly they turned a sharp corner. Before she could protest, she found herself being placed in a rowboat.

"What are you doing? Where are we going?"

"Sit down, *Signorina*. I fear our ruse was not quite as convincing as I had hoped. If we are quick, we can lose them."

He pushed the boat off and began rowing with long strokes that sliced through the top of the water with a vengeance. He rowed for a good five minutes toward Venice proper, this time Gwendolyn was the one watching over her shoulder, but for what or whom, she did not know.

A few more minutes went by then she saw them. A small vessel full of people cutting across the canal, far away yet, but the blackguards were most definitely in pursuit.

"There's a boat!" she warned him.

"I see it. We are almost there."

The longest single minute or so of Gwendolyn's life dragged by as he rowed their boat across the canal with the strength of ten men. He drove them up a narrow waterway, passing under a few bridges. He made a couple of turns then finally their little boat scraped alongside a jetty. He jumped out and hauled her out as if she were a rag doll.

They ran around a few more corners, but their pursuers continued to close in on her and her companion.

"I thought we had lost them," she whispered, edging closer to uncertainty mixed with fear.

"This way." He led her over a bridge and down a long walkway until they came to a drop off, where there was only water at the end, no bridge for them to escape over.

"Do you swim?"

Panic shocked through her body. "Of course."

"Come." And he pulled her into the filthy canal.

Gwendolyn came up gagging on the putrid water. Her new wig was most likely on its way to the bottom.

With a point of a finger, he indicated a bridge not far off and they swam for the shelter it created, trying not to splash as they moved through the dank, fetid passage.

At first her skirts stayed up around her waist, allowing her legs to propel her forward, but all too soon the fabric plummeted to impede her ankles as it drank in what the canal had to offer.

Gwendolyn stalled in the very center and an involuntary squeak escaped her throat. The more she struggled, the more she sank, lower and lower until her face was the only thing peering up from the cruel baptismal. She gulped for air as if it would be her final endeavor in this life.

In moments, her fellow fugitive hauled her to his side, moving both of them through the cold water with such ease it took her aback.

She clung to him shivering, concealed beneath a stone bridge.

As they watched from the frigid canal in the darkest of shadows, they observed the men peer out from between buildings on the opposite side.

As if deciding they had taken the wrong corridor, their pursuers retreated.

Frozen to the bone, she barely noticed when her companion lifted himself out of the water then reached in, hoisting Gwendolyn in her saturated gown up and out. Without pause, he took her by the hand and they began to run again, passing through quaint squares. Gwendolyn had a difficult time running in her sodden skirts and the sharp wind blew mercilessly as if attempting to impede their flight.

The walkway widened and they found themselves racing through Piazza San Marco beneath the corridor that flanked the south side.

Finally arriving at the east side of the square, they crossed the Piazzetta, to the Doge's palace, where he stopped at an iron gate. He awakened the guard with a few brisk Italian sentences and they were admitted. Once he made sure the gate was locked, they took another flight of stairs and crossed the long terrace. On the far side of the square, they could see the men who had been searching for them. Although Gwendolyn was certain they'd left a wet trail behind them during their escape from the canal, it seemed the men weren't concerned with the ground, only windows and shop entrances. Her companion held tightly to her hand as they went. They turned a corner and stepped through a doorway.

To Gwendolyn's mortified surprise, there was a party going on, and she was hauled before the Doge of Venice, soaked through to her skin and smelling like a sewer. Thank goodness her soggy half-mask yet clung to her face, concealing the discomfiture beneath. Glancing up, she noticed that her companion's mask was misshapen from their impromptu swim, but he still hadn't removed it.

Gwendolyn curtsied when he introduced her in Italian—the two men's familiarity blazingly obvious, even with the added language barrier. She had no idea what everyone was saying, but smiled nonetheless. She looked around and was barely able to take note of the opulence of the room when she was once again being relocated to another staircase. They climbed to the next floor, and closed the door behind them. Then they hurried down another lengthy hallway, and through yet another portal into a dark room.

A servant, a short, older man, came in behind them and lit candles set upon table tops and shelves. Gwendolyn realized the bedroom served as their sanctuary. The servant spoke to her companion in Italian, who in turn thanked him.

When the man left, he turned to Gwendolyn and she waited for him to speak, as they had not communicated in a normal fashion since they'd jumped into the freezing canal.

When he finally spoke it wasn't nearly enough to satisfy her aching curiosity and racing heart. "My apologies."

* * * *

A soft moan escaped Ellie's lips when Weston's fingers found their mark. She closed her eyes and floated atop the mounting wave that all but consumed her.

"Now it is your turn to tell me," he whispered, his hand never faltering.

"Wha—" Somewhere in the back of her mind she accepted the fact that she wasn't able to form a complete word, but she couldn't have cared less. She was with Weston, naked, and he was touching her so skillfully she could have died right there with a deep sense of bliss.

And for heaven's sake, she wasn't in the mood for a discussion.

"Tell me how you like to be touched."

"Mm."

"Ellie?"

"Hm?"

"Should I stop so you can concentrate on our conversation?"

Her eyes flew open. "No, no, don't stop, Weston, please."

She heard him chuckle. "Then tell me how you like it," he said and nipped at her earlobe.

Ellie licked her lips. "Well, what are my options?"

Weston barely paused in his petting and changed the course of his hand. "I could do it this way." He pressed his middle finger down gently and swept over her pearl, forcing to the right, then to the left, and back again, over and over while Ellie panted at the sensation.

He stole the breath from her words. "Oooh, that's nice."

"And there is this." Again he altered directions, and softly stroked her up and down with the same insistent rhythm and gentle pressure.

"Oooh!" she moaned, her hips rocking a bit.

"How about this way?" The tips of his fingers surrounded her straining flesh he tugged gently at it, still keeping to that wicked tempo of his.

"Yes." She panted. "Oh, that's so good!"

"And of course, you already know this one." He altered the focus of his fingers and drew the little circles she was so fond of last time.

Her breath held as the wave built to a crescendo and he stopped.

Ellie lifted her head, a protest tumbling from her lips. "No! You can't stop now!"

"You have to tell me which way you like it."

"All of it, any of it. Oh hurry!"

He grinned at her. "There is another way. I have saved the best for last."

Ellie's eyes widened. There couldn't be anything better than what he had been doing, could there be?

* * * *

"I beg your pardon?" Gwendolyn blinked at him as she felt the shivers coming on once again.

"I'm afraid I have dragged you into my troubles."

"Nonsense. Those men could not have known who I am," she said, her jaw trembling.

He took up a blanket from the end of a bed and enclosed her in its warmth. "They know. Trust me," he said with foreboding, giving her shoulders a squeeze.

Gwendolyn would have harrumphed at Mr. Elusive asking her to trust him, but she was too cold to care.

A knock came at the door. Not a moment later, at least fifteen servants carrying large buckets of steaming water entered the room and continued through another door.

Retrieving a glass from a sideboard, he then poured her some brandy and pressed the glass into her free hand. She drank it down quickly to avoid the burn.

"I would have thought that a lady would not be fond of brandy," he commented as he tossed a large amount back himself.

"My father kept a decanter in his study. I used to stick my finger into it as if it were a cone of sugar."

Grinning, he splashed more into her vessel.

When the servants finally took their leave, he indicated to the open door. "After you," he offered, and removed the empty vessel from her hand.

Gwendolyn picked up one of the three-arm brass candlesticks from atop a bureau. Once inside the room, she found a vanity with a large mirror, a tall wardrobe, an ornate stool, a washbasin and pitcher, and a huge tiled bath. The steam rose and disappeared into the tall ceiling, beckoning to her, promising her a satisfying warmth if she would but slip inside the hot water. Letting the blanket fall into a puddle at her feet, she then set the candle on the vanity and began stripping the ruined dress and underpinnings from her body, ripping seams here and there of the now worthless gown. She tossed the stinking lot into a corner then pealed the soggy mask from her face and added it to the pile.

Finally rid of every fabric hindrance, Gwendolyn held onto the side and carefully dipped a foot into the water. It was almost too hot. Hissing, she turned to look over her shoulder, thinking she had forgotten something.

He stood in the open door, leaning on the frame. The first thing she noticed was his bare chest. The second was his face.

His *maskless* face.

And he was, without a doubt, the most beautiful man she had ever seen.

Chapter Fourteen

Before Ellie could think of what could possibly feel better, Weston slid down her body and placed his mouth where it just shouldn't have been.

"Weston, what are you—?" Ellie couldn't help herself. She moaned so loud it sounded like a shriek to her ears.

His lips were hot and wet as it teased her rigid nub, his fingers spreading her flesh wide to get at it. She dragged great gulps of air into her lungs as his slick mouth did delicious things between her thighs. His tongue was quick as he wiggled and poked at her pearl repeatedly, then at intervals, dipped down lower to where Ellie felt moisture gathering at an alarming rate. She trapped a deep breath in her lungs as she could no longer stand the sweet torture. Then, as if he could sense her crisis, he covered her completely with his fevered mouth and sucked mercilessly on her, causing her to release her breath in a loud moan, but stopping just in time for his tongue to dip down again. His rhythm was driving her to the point of insanity, and she never wanted it to end.

It did end though, and Ellie thought she was going to die from the pleasure. Her body jolted as she shouted her ecstasy, and still he sucked at her, holding her hips, crushing his mouth to her.

Within a blink of an eye, he moved between her legs and bent his head to one of her nipples.

Ellie was buzzing with sensation when he entered her. She gripped his shoulders when she felt the pain-pleasure of the sting between her legs as her body gave way to his intrusion.

* * * *

Gwendolyn realized, all too late, that she had forgotten to close off the entrance. Her cheeks burned with mortification. When he stepped farther into the room and shut the door behind him, she turned from him and slipped into the tub, mortified that he had witnessed her disrobing—not to mention her nude body. She took a deep breath and sank under the hot water in embarrassment.

Gwendolyn felt the water swell around her and came up sputtering. He had joined her. "What are you doing?" she cried, sweeping wisps of wet hair from her eyes, and curling up in a ball at one end of the tub.

"What do you think I'm doing?"

Gwendolyn grimaced and conceded that her question was rather obtuse. He grinned at her, just before ducking under the water.

Letting her guard down for the briefest of moments, she felt her eyes widen. Even with his hair plastered to his face from their swim in the canal, he was stunning to look upon. He was even more handsome than she had imagined him to be when they did all but fornicate in that confessional box. She knew this man, and yet she didn't. It was enough to make a person run mad.

He came up and squeezed the water from his hair. Gwendolyn couldn't take her eyes from him. His beautiful, large dark-brown gaze burned with a sensual intensity that left her insides swirling like the steam that rose from the water of their bath. The skin on his well-muscled arms and shoulders was a deep, tanned olive tone, not pasty like most of the men in London.

"Gwendolyn, what is going through your mind?" he asked, shaking her from her musings.

"That I-I don't even know you."

He sighed. "Ah, that again."

"Yes *that* again." She scolded him as if he were a little boy who was found repeatedly pilfering sweets and knew better. "Here you sit in *my* bath, invading *my* privacy and you don't even have the decency to introduce yourself!"

"I had thought the open door to be an invitation—"

She interrupted him by shaking a dripping finger in his face. "Don't you dare punish me for forgetting to close that door! If you had even a shred of decency—"

He held up his wet hands in surrender. "I concede, *Signorina*." He chuckled.

His dimpled grin sent a shock wave from her breasts to the juncture of her thighs and spread warmly through her stomach. His features were so striking, she couldn't help the reaction. Covering the awkwardness she felt from the sensation, she lowered her arm and spoke. "That's much better. Now, what is your name?"

After a pause that she thought would precede yet another denial of information, he spoke. "I am Marcello Anthony Verdante."

His voice was quiet and low when he'd said his name, as if it were an expletive. The sound coupled with his accent sent a thrill up her spine. She dared not say his name aloud. Who knew what it would do to the rest of her body? She licked her lips at the thought and his gaze dropped to her mouth as she did so.

"Are you not going to exchange polite salutations with me?"

"What would you require, a handshake—or shall I curtsy?" She nearly laughed at her own jest however sobered just as quickly. "Seriously, you must be joking. We are unclothed and close enough to touch." *Now where in the world had that come from?*

He shrugged an ample shoulder. "Correct again, *Signorina.*"

She hadn't a moment to enjoy her triumph, because Marcello had reached out, dragged her toward him and reclined against the slanted back of the tub. She felt her eyes go wide as her body floated over his, only touching when one of them moved.

"This is much better."

Gwendolyn went to move away with a sharp intake of breath, but the length of her pressed against his. She had been so foolish she could have kicked herself in the backside. Who was she to think that he would leave her to her privacy? Not to mention that if he would allow *her* to leave the room, he would probably watch as she rose from the tub, and for the second time that evening, nothing would hide her naked body from his gaze. She sucked the inside of her cheek between her teeth as she contemplated her next move.

Marcello reached out and took a cake of soap from a tiny shelf which protruded from the tiles. Gwendolyn felt the soap being drawn over her bottom.

She almost rose out of the water to object, when one of his knees lifted between her legs. Amidst her sputtering protests, he held her there and soaped her as if she were incapable. *The audacity! The utter nerve!* But God... How it drew her desires to the surface of her awareness. She fought with every shred of determination she possessed not to rub her throbbing womanhood against his leg. It was enough that he seemed to press his thigh harder against her with every stroke of the soap.

"This is very undignified, sir," she said, trying to hold her body still and quite unsuccessfully so. "I am a grown woman, able to bathe myself."

He had the gall to chuckle at her. "Turn over, *Signorina*, I have not finished."

"I beg to differ, sir, you have indeed fin—"

He flipped her over as if she were a leaf in the wind, his knee coming up once again between her thighs.

Gwendolyn gasped as she looked down at her nude body lying atop his, her legs on either side of his thickly muscled thigh, watching as his hands worked vigorously at the cake of soap. She suspected that he had sinister plans for the lather he was creating. It made her shiver to imagine what he was going to do with it.

* * * *

Wes paused just after he felt Ellie's body yield to his. "Are you all right?" he whispered, suddenly fearful she may have been hurt.

"I don't think"—she panted—"I've ever been better." He could hear the smile in her voice.

God, but she was tight—and so wet, but now that the initial path had been established and her virgin's barrier eliminated, she would feel little discomfort, if any, provided he was gentle. He eased himself in and out slowly at first, Ellie's hips fervently undulated, meeting his strokes, likely by sheer instinct. Her soft sighs were enough to send him over the edge.

"Ellie—" Wes hadn't meant for his voice to sound like a plea, but it did.

"Yes," she moaned in that utterly feminine way of hers.

He wanted Ellie to have the best experience, to never forget her first time. He wanted her to see him from across a crowded room and remember how his body fit perfectly with hers, how he'd made her come so easily and how she'd cried out when she did. Just then, he did something he'd only heard about. He reached down between their bodies and began manipulating her pearl as he stroked her from within.

Ellie went off like a shot, singing her ecstasy as she rode her orgasm, her inner muscles working his cock as if in punishment for torturing her so pleasantly. Wes reached up and smoothed his hand over one of her plump breasts, pulled out and came on her belly, echoing her sentiment. He still rubbed the base of his cock between her legs as she continued to come, which elongated his own blinding culmination. His breath caught as he ground himself into her, feeling as if he was coming a second time, and it pleased him immensely. None of the other women he'd lain with had been able to do to him what Ellie had. If he wasn't shaking so hard from his efforts, he would have shouted his triumph.

When her shuddering diminished, he lowered himself to the bed next to her and held her tenderly.

His body was covered with a fine sheen of sweat. The coolness in the room made him shiver. It had been the most amazing sexual encounter he'd ever had, and he would be a fool if he did not ask her to marry him before they left for home. It wasn't only the sex, which was beyond extraordinary, but he loved her, cared about her. They had things in common that he hadn't even known about until they took this holiday together. His heart constricted at the thought. He placed a kiss on her damp temple and she sighed. Had he loved her all along?

In a word, yes. He grinned.

Chapter Fifteen

Marcello placed the soap back onto the shelf and lifted Gwendolyn with his body so that she was well out of the water. He smoothed his hands over her breasts and belly. Then when he delved his soapy hand between her legs, she let out a moan that echoed off the tiled walls of the small room.

She watched as he played. He wove his fingers into her triangle of curling hairs then combed the lather out of the way until her clitoris peeked out and retreated again, over and over, driving her simply mad. God, but she wanted him to touch it, to swirl it between his strong fingers.

As if reading her mind, he slid his digits down either side of her excited nub. Gwendolyn's hips moved from side to side as if by their own accord, begging him to take hold of her flesh.

"I know what you want, *mia dolce ciliegia.*" His voice rumbled in her ears, sending her already hard, soapy nipples to peak and tingle. She shivered.

Marcelo must have noticed the tips of her breasts pucker further. With one of his hands, he grazed her nipples while with the other he pushed her lower body under the water to rinse the soap away. He toyed with her, inadvertently removing the layer of lather, until she was a ball of sensation.

God, she needed him to bring her to an explosive end.

At once, he sat her upright in front of him. Much to her embarrassment, she made a squeak of protest and turned to him. Had he not been so handsome, she might have told him a thing or two, regardless of the devil's own grin on his face.

"Wash your hair, *Signorina*," he said, and reached for the cake of soap from the shelf. Breaking off a piece, he then handed the larger portion to Gwendolyn. When he began to soap his hair, she turned her back to him.

She heard the tinkling of the water behind her. He must have been washing himself. Gwendolyn's cheeks burned with a furious fire. She should take him to task for seducing her in this vulgar manner. However, much to her shame, she wanted more. Why hadn't he finished her off the way he had last time? The feeling in her stomach was ebbing, but the concentrated pressure between her legs begged for release. She scrubbed her scalp vigorously in her frustration.

She felt the water level lower. He must have gotten out. Gwendolyn turned her head just enough to see that he was now standing with his back to her in front of the tall wardrobe. He opened the wide, ornate doors.

Observing him, her gaze traveled from the top of his dark hair to where it ended clinging and wet on the back of his neck, then slid to his wide shoulders, down his muscled back to his narrow hips. A shot of excitement went through her as she took in the sight of his naked bottom. *How lovely*. Curved and dented in on each side, his buttocks sat upon his legs indolently, as if they knew how beautiful they were. She wanted to touch them, to experience the difference between when he was flexing and when he was relaxed.

His body had been still for as long as she had been watching him. She glanced at the open doors of the wardrobe, where inside hung long mirrors. With an intake of breath, she locked gazes with his in one of the mirrors. He was watching her with an intensity that gave off a heat she could feel from where she sat. She turned away and made herself busy with finding the two pieces of severed soap. Putting them together, she then placed them on the shelf.

"You seemed to have missed a spot." The sound of his deep voice rolled down her back

She turned to him, still feverish and shy even after everything he had done with her body, everything she had let him do. He now had a drying sheet wrapped around his waist, the end of it flung over his shoulder, Greco-Roman-style. He knelt next to the tub and reached for her hair.

"Lie back, let me help you."

Gwendolyn did as she'd been told. He bade her tilt her head back and dip the top into the water. He massaged and rinsed the soap from her hair. She closed her eyes, the sensation relaxing her so much, she didn't want to move. All too soon, she felt his hands leave her scalp. She opened her eyes and lifted her head. He was leaning on the side of the tub, his gaze wandering over her body that lay just beneath the surface of the water. It was rather dark with only the three flames of the candles, but she knew he could see every curve. As she watched him looking at her, that insistent pressure at the juncture of her thighs made her wish he would reach out and finish what he'd started.

Touch me. Slip your fingers between my legs and ease my torture. She knew her wicked thoughts shown in her gaze and she blinked them away, the heat of her blush now rising from her entire body.

He held his hand out to her and she took it, swallowing the thoughts that were threatening to emerge from her lips. He pulled her to a sitting position, her breasts exposed to his sight once again. From next to him on the floor, he took a drying sheet and stood, holding it up for her.

It only took a moment for Gwendolyn to stand and lean into his offering. Marcello wrapped it around her body and proceeded to rub his hands up and down her arms, then her back, drying her and warming her at the same time.

He unwrapped her just enough for her to lift her arms out. He replaced the fabric and tucked in the top.

More decently covered than she had been just before her bath, she felt she could look him in the face again. She turned to him and raised her gaze to his.

* * * *

Ellie's eyelids drooped to a close and she drifted off to a light sleep. She awoke when Weston left the bed and she turned to watch him cross the room. He went to the washbasin and dipped a linen cloth into the water. He brought in back, and she marveled at him as he wiped his semen from her belly. It was terribly thoughtful of him. She smiled up at him dreamily.

Weston winked at Ellie and tossed the used rag into a corner.

"I'm a bit chilled."

"What? After all that exercise?" He grinned crookedly at her.

She giggled.

"Come on then. Let me get you under the covers."

While Ellie climbed between the sheets, Weston fetched an extra mantle that had been draped across the back of a nearby chair. "Here," he said as he covered her tenderly with it. He made her feel so cherished.

She caught his hand. "Stay with me."

"But what if Gwen—"

"It's early yet. Gwennie won't be back for hours." She grimaced inwardly at the desperate tone of her voice. It was true, though, and besides that, she didn't want him to go. Not ever. It was bad enough that once they arrived in London, he was sure to forget about her. He would go back to being a bachelor, and she would be tossed to the wolves of the marriage market. Her family wasn't titled, but her fortune made her a prime target for some fund-depleted old lord. Her ponderings nearly brought tears to her eyes.

"I think that even if you wanted me gone, you would have to convince me to leave." He grinned.

Ellie couldn't help but smile at his words. She scooted over in invitation.

Weston slid into the covers. Ellie giggled when he growled and reached for her.

* * * *

Gwendolyn observed Marcello's hair. It hung in stringy, dripping waves and fell over his forehead, framing his handsome face. Her view was blocked as he covered her head with a small drying towel. He lifted her hair and enfolded its length in the linen, wringing out the water.

The sheet slid from her head. "Thank you," she murmured.

Marcello didn't seem to hear her. He tossed the linen aside and drew her through the door back into the bedroom. A hearth she hadn't noticed before sported wild orangey-red flames which made the room smell of burning wood. Where in the world the Venetians acquired peat and logs when no forest grew in the vicinity was beyond her.

He maneuvered her next to the fireplace, where the heat warmed the drying sheet in which she was wrapped. She felt his palms run up and down her sides, adding to the warmth. She remembered his hands on her body while he'd bathed her in the most erotic way she could ever have imagined, his soapy digits sliding down to cleanse her secret woman's place that still ached for his touch. But the area between her legs was no longer a secret, was it? No. Since she had known him, she'd allowed Marcello Verdante's hands, fingers and even his mouth to play on her. She shuddered when she recalled how his tongue skillfully teased her—how he sucked on her and how he made her die with the pleasure of it.

He spoke, bringing Gwendolyn out of her thoughts. "They will be watching for us, you know," he said, still rubbing her upper arms.

"Hm, who?"

"The men who were chasing me. I fear we are to be detained here for the duration of the night."

She nodded. "I understand." Honestly, she felt they were safe from their pursuers, at least until they attempted to leave the safety of the Doge's palace.

Gwendolyn stared into the fire. Tonight, would he put his hands on her again, his lips, his mouth? They were all alone, protected by the Doge of Venice and his guards. The large four-poster bed loomed behind them, calling to her...to them.

He briefly caressed her upper back. The simple action promised Gwendolyn that she would taste pleasure again before the sun rose. It was either accept his attentions this night or never experience the merging of souls with this man. She swallowed her anxiety and glanced at him from the corner of her eye. God help her, she wanted him to take her and make love to her no matter how devastating the outcome. Her ruination would likely be the most pleasurable experience of her life. The irony stung like a slap. To have a lover this beautifully masculine, this powerful, someone who made her heart race sent a shuddering thrill through her body.

Pity it could never work between them. It seemed he had dangerous, unrelenting enemies—who knew for how long he'd have to run? Gwendolyn regretted that the moment it was safe, she must leave Venice, never to return. Marcello would not likely try to find her. She would go back and face the marriage market with Ellie and make the best of it. That is, if anyone would have her after this night.

"Are you warm enough?" he asked.

There was no way he could have read her thoughts. She nodded.

"There is no need to fear. I will sleep on the floor."

Gwendolyn turned to Marcello and his hands fell to his sides.

"That will be unnecessary," she said and lifted the drying sheet as if it were a skirt, so that she could walk over to the bed somewhat dignified. She only paused when he spoke.

"You wish for me to sleep with you?"

She could hear the question mixed with awe. Gwendolyn turned her head and, observing the uncertain anticipation on his face, nodded regally.

Chapter Sixteen

Ellie was amazed at all the wonderful things Weston's manly bits were capable of. As he'd promised, she had been allowed to play with him, unhindered by rules and time limits. Before she'd begun to touch him, she'd caught him unawares. He was soft, un-intimidating, even peaceful. But now, after she had explored the mysteries of the man who lay next to her, his manhood grew at an alarming rate. It became almost hot to the touch, demanding and effectively daunting as it stretched toward her, as if it knew exactly what it wanted. It excited her terribly to think that the movement of her hands was the key to his secret place and the door which was about to be thrown open yet again.

"Would you like to taste me?" he whispered.

She looked up at him. "Can I do that?"

He chuckled, but his voice seemed pained. "You can do anything you'd like."

She thought for a second on how she wanted to approach this. "Stand up next to the bed."

He slid from the beneath the covers and stood before her. God, but he was beautiful, so tall and firm, she loved the way the muscles curved over his shoulders and arms. Briefly, she glanced down. His part, which she'd been in awe of, thrust high and proud in front of him, insolent and demanding her attention.

Terribly excited about what she was about to do, Ellie tossed aside the covers and climbed out of the bed. She circled him then came to a kneeling position on the floor before him.

He was still a bit tall for her, so he spread his feet apart a step or two. He was now right in front of her mouth, so substantial—threatening even—and yet so beautiful.

Timidly, she took hold of him and opened her lips. With her tongue she licked at the tip. She heard his breath catch, and it encouraged her. She lapped at the length of him, toying with the tight sac between his legs. A boldness swept over her and she slowly took him into her mouth as far as she could. She then closed her lips around him. Using her hands, she reached under to smooth her fingers up and down his glorious bottom. She smiled inwardly as he groaned as loudly as she had when he did this sort of thing to her. She answered him with a closed-lipped groan of her own and his breath caught yet again. She must have been doing something right.

But she wasn't finished with him, yet. She sucked on him just a bit then slid him from her mouth.

"Ellie, don't stop," he growled deep in his throat.

"I have one more thing I wish to try." She went to the dresser and retrieved the bottle of rose oil she'd purchased from the perfumery earlier that day. She proceeded to slather the oil between her breasts. Then she turned the bottle upside down over his manly part, dripping the oil out and massaging it into his skin.

Oh, she knew she was doing this right, too. His breathing came in audible gasps, now. She bade him lay on the bed on his back, then she hovered over him. Taking her breasts in her hands, she then surrounded him, mixing the oil on his skin with the oil on hers. Ellie sighed, enjoying the feeling of him delving into her cleavage, knowing she pleasured him just as much. She could almost hear him gasping her name with each gentle thrust.

"God, Ellie, you've gotten me so stiff, I can hardly stand it."

Quickly, she reached for the oil again, this time she poured a healthy amount into her hand. She rubbed her palms together then grasped him. She began sliding her hands up and down his thick shaft just like he had shown her. He was gloriously hard and hot in her hands.

"El, I can't wait anymore. I need to come —"

"Yes, Weston. Come!" she moaned and leaned over him, covering him with her hands and breasts.

Weston came long and hard — the evidence of it soaking her from neck to chest. She hadn't let go of him, it was too sweet a victory to relinquish her hold just yet.

He squirmed a bit. "I'm so sensitive now, you have to let me go," he uttered, his voice just above a whisper.

He let out a bit of a yelp as he slipped through her hands. She'd done it on purpose, of course, savoring her triumph. She grinned. She wanted to shout. It appeared she had given him the same kind of pleasure he had given her. It felt to her as if she had a new understanding of the male anatomy, and it was a heady feeling.

Ellie got up and cleaned herself at the washbasin. She was shaking, most likely due to her efforts.

She rearranged the covers over the two of them, and after she was settled, much to her surprise, he set his hand between her thighs.

"Have you not had enough?" she asked breathlessly when he closed his fingers over her taunt pearl.

"I have. You haven't."

"What is that supposed to mean?" she moaned, wishing she could protest, but she felt so swollen between his fingers, she thought she would burst.

"Does something feel different as I am touching you right now?" he asked and began those maddening little circles of his.

"Yes. Oh, it's so good. It... It's so hot and... I don't know how to describe..." she panted, forcing out her words. She could barely breathe let alone speak.

"Do you feel a heaviness here, right now, more so than usual?"

"Yes, that is it," she squeaked as she breathed in great gulping breaths.

"Is it a sweet, insistent pressure that you can hardly stand?"

Ellie nodded frantically.

"You are hard, just as I was, my Ellie," he breathed into her ear and nipped at her earlobe. "Playing with me the way you did, made the blood rush to this very place." He indicated by gently wiggling her straining flesh a few times.

"Y-yes," she panted, that must have been the case, for it did excite her terribly to touch him, to watch him enjoy his pleasure.

Suddenly, he was between her legs. She felt his lips close over the spot which seemed to beg for more stimulation.

Ellie turned her head and screamed into her pillow as she came — and came. And came.

Weston slid a finger into her opening as she rocked her hips, demanding he delve deeper. As if not wishing to disappoint her, he rose over her and plunged inside before her orgasms ebbed. She seemed to burst from the inside and mindlessly clawed at his back as he rode her.

It was magnificent — like staring into the sun.

Weston knew he should quit the room soon, but he curled up next to Ellie regardless.

She rolled toward him, draped an arm over his stomach and sighed contentedly.

He grinned and closed his eyes. She'd given him so much tonight, both physically and emotionally. He turned his head toward her and inhaled. Her feminine powdery fragrance was now mixed with rose and the musky scent of their lovemaking. Weston's smile widened and he snuggled closer to his Ellie. He counted himself the happiest man alive.

Together they drifted off to sleep, shutting out the world, comfortable in their cozy nest.

* * * *

Gwendolyn was not two steps from the bed when Marcello dragged her back to the fireplace by the back of her drying sheet.

"Very well, we shall sleep, but not until I have had a chance to see you in the light."

"Take this off." He indicated the fabric.

She complied and waited as he piled pillows in front of the fireplace, then covered them with a thick blanket.

When he was finished cushioning the floor before the fire, he turned to her and froze. He was finally able to see her without shadows covering her, and she was indeed beautiful. For all her girlish trembling, she'd succumbed in his arms. She had the curves of a woman. Her hips were round, her legs long and strong looking, and her breasts...

Taking her by the hand, Marcello guided Gwendolyn onto the makeshift bed and had her face the fire. He stood behind her and bade her kneel. She did, and he settled himself behind her, his bent knees between hers. He spread her buttocks and pressed himself, pointing downward, between the cheeks of her lush round bottom. Her soft flesh surrounding his hard cock felt glorious. He swept her damp hair from her neck and tossed it over his left shoulder.

"Now reach behind, and place your hands on my legs."

Gwendolyn placed her hands on his muscled thighs. They were hard, thoroughly masculine. She felt the heat of the fire on her skin and from behind, his warmth seared her, the length of his manhood lay just at the opening of her bottom. As warm as she was, her nipples puckered.

With his head bent over her shoulder, she noticed how he watched her body while his hands went to work, skimming over her skin, sending waves of sensation to her core.

She felt weak. He was so good at being all over her at once. She closed her eyes and tilted her head back, resting on his shoulder. He could do anything he wanted to her. Tonight she was his.

When she felt his fingers spread her flesh, exposing her clitoris to the fire, her eyes snapped opened on their own and her breath caught in her throat.

"Can you feel the heat, *mia ciliegia*?" he asked as he slid his fingers toward her nub. "It is far hotter than my tongue, and I am jealous the fire can see you, can smell you, can burn you."

A whimper escaped her. God, when would he take hold of her? When would he give her that devastating pleasure he spoke of? For a few aching moments, he didn't move, but he continued whispering sinful things in her ear.

"I know what you want, and I know how to give you what you desire."

His wicked promises were about to drive her mad. "Please," she whispered harshly.

"This tiny piece of your body" — he began to tap at her swollen flesh with an index finger — "holds more power than you can imagine. It has the ability to send shockwaves through you." He tapped harder. "And when I touch it, all I want to do is take it into my mouth and suck until you come."

Gwendolyn's bottom tensed, squeezing him between her buttock cheeks and Marcello groaned. He leaned backward a bit, arching her upper body away from the heat, her lower body toward it and rubbing himself along the slickness between her legs.

"Even the fire wants to lick you, to lick your sweet *ciliegia*," he took her nub between his fingers and began twisting it back and forth.

She could hardly draw enough air into her lungs she was panting so hard. He was wicked. His sinful fingers brought her to dizzying heights. He was a dark

Italian devil, and she wanted him to take her, right here, amidst the fires of hell.

Marcello's hips were rocking hers closer to the fire. "If these flames could suck you, they would reach out and take you between their lips. Can you feel their heat?"

Gwendolyn moaned in response. Suddenly she was on her back, a stack of pillows raising her hips toward the ceiling. Marcello buried his mouth into her flesh and sucked at her hard. Just when she thought she could no longer take his attentions, he pressed his lips to her more firmly, quivering his head from side to side, shaking not only her pearl, but the fleshy mound around it.

She could no longer withstand the pleasurable sensation. She burst into a million stars and cried out, the sound of her ecstasy filling the room.

Chapter Seventeen

Clinging to her with an intense suction, Marcello stilled his movements, his ears ringing from her lusty cries. He felt her shudder with the last waves of her orgasm and slowly let her slip from his mouth. Tentatively, he slid the tip of his finger into her. She was ripe, slick and her body beckoned to him to sink his cock deep within her.

Gwendolyn's virginity was a bit of a problem. He'd been lucky that the few virgins who gave up their prize to him had not felt but a slight pain. Perhaps he knew what he was doing. Perhaps he would let Gwendolyn control the coupling.

Marcello rose, scooped her up and set her upon the bed. She was a limp as a rag doll from his play. Quickly, he replaced the pillows he'd tossed to the floor to the head of the bed, where he stacked them and settled himself against their softness.

He knew Gwendolyn had been watching him from hooded eyes. "Come," Marcello reached out to her and pulled her atop him, her legs on either side of his thighs. He guided her bottom so that his cock was leaning against the light curls between her legs.

Gwendolyn's hips rocked forward and back, rubbing herself against him, as if giving him permission to take her. Marcello groaned.

Countering her rocking, he tilted his hips so that his tip caught in her wet opening. He heard her sharp intake of breath and made to sooth her.

"Shh, *mia dolce*," he said, sweeping her hair back over her shoulder. "Take me inside you, slowly. When it becomes uncomfortable, stop."

Gwendolyn nodded once, and he watched as her eyebrows drew together in concentration.

She is so courageous, he thought as he kept his desire at bay. It took every ounce of effort not to spike himself into her. This slowness would probably kill him.

She began the agonizingly deliberate descent down his cock, and he closed his eyes, not being able to endure the stirring sight of her efforts.

When she finally paused, he opened his eyes. The look on her face was uncertain. She was almost half way down and must have stretched her barrier significantly.

"Are you all right?"

She nodded, but didn't make a move to go any farther.

He slid his hand up the tops of her thighs. "Is it very painful?"

Gwendolyn shrugged a shoulder, "Just a bit unpleasant, is all."

"Let me ease you a little."

Marcello glided his fingers toward her exposed pearl.

Gwendolyn closed her eyes when he began teasing her still-swollen flesh with his fingers. Her head tilted back on its own. God, but he knew exactly how to handle her—how to draw her to the edge of oblivion over and over again.

She let herself relax, and another thick inch or two was consumed by her body. Her insides squeezed at the intrusion, extracting a moan from Marcello. She gazed at her lover. His head was thrown back as well, resting against the pillows at his back while he played with her. Gwendolyn squeezed her inner muscles again and Marcello's jaw went slack.

She grinned.

His fingers became insistent, and she was nearing another pull of the tides. She could swear she felt her nub pulsate against his teasing digits. When the first wave hit, she convulsed and slid down to his hilt. Her virgin's barrier was now fully breached, but she barely noticed as he embraced her frenzied flesh with his fingers. Her body arched and writhed as she voiced her pleasure, Marcello still plying his torture. Her insides convulsed around him and when his hands finally stilled, she fell forward, catching herself before fully collapsing on top of him.

Marcello slid his arms around her, hugging her close. "Gwendolyn?" he whispered his inquiry.

On shaking arms, she pushed herself away just enough to look into his eyes. She smiled shyly.

Marcello lifted a damp lock of hair that had fallen over her shoulder. He glanced down to gaze at her cleavage. She felt him jump inside her. She squeezed him back in return.

His slow grin prompted her to lean down and kiss him.

He took her by the hips and shifted under her, pressing his pelvis forward. She gasped at the sensation and shuddered.

That was it. Gwendolyn Rawleigh, his little English virgin, with the most perfect body he'd ever been buried to the hilt in, was about to drive him mad. He guided her and showed her how to find that spot up inside her that sent shivers through her body. He hit it again and she lost her breath.

"What is that?" she whispered in wonder.

"It is me writing my name inside you," he replied and groaned as he tilted himself into her.

After a few more strokes, he zeroed in on the tiny spot. With well-practiced precision, he angled his thrusts inside her so that every thrust hit it with blinding accuracy.

Gwendolyn was singing her excitement again, and Marcello could stand it no longer. He let go of her and slid his hands to her breasts, his hips bucking as he thrust into her. The shattering orgasm rocked his body, his soul.

Gwendolyn collapsed onto his chest then, her breathing ragged as it tried to catch up with the pounding of her heart that competed against his own.

Marcello stroked his hand down Gwendolyn's long, damp hair, and gathered it into one hand. He braided it loosely and laid it down the center of her spine. From atop his chest, Gwendolyn inhaled and heaved an unladylike sigh. He grinned. "Sleep now, *mia dolce pocociligia*," he whispered. "We only have an hour or so to be at peace."

Gwendolyn reached up and scratched her nose, then nuzzled his chest with her cheek.

* * * *

Albert paced between the Doge's palace and the Canal of San Marco, also keeping an eye on the side of the structure which flanked the Piazzetta. The Florentine men whom he'd contacted had responded precipitously when they received his note about the suspicious actions of a tall, rich-looking man, but had returned angry from the private garden into which they had followed the fellow.

He remembered how they'd argued with him about the man in the garden.

"*Signore* Pedley, I'm telling you," the Florentine badgered. "That was not Marcello Verdante!"

Albert looked incredulously at the men. "Impossible."

"It was some Englishman taking his new bride for a tumble in a garden."

Albert would have sworn on a stack of bibles that the man who had ventured into that garden and had been watching Wes's sister Gwendolyn for nearly twelve hours now, was Marcello Verdante. He'd fit the description, as vague as it had been, perfectly. He was positive that snobby Miss Rawleigh had led the wanted man right into Albert's hands. And what payback that would have been to deny her of a lover.

He didn't blame this Marcello Verdante, really. Any healthy man, in possession of all his functions, would want to pursue the sassy, haughty Gwendolyn Rawleigh.

"How do you know he was an Englishman?" he growled.

"They spoke to us, *Signore*, and his accent was much like yours. However, I think his bride must have been from somewhere else."

He narrowed his eyes at the second man and spoke slowly, as if each word were its own sentence. "What makes you say that?"

"Her speech was odd."

Irritated, Albert probed for more information on the exchange. "Odd, how? What did she say?"

The two men looked at each other before one of them spoke. "The *signora* began her sentence with 'och,' but I did not understand the words she said next."

Albert clenched his teeth before he spoke, and when he did so, his voice was low and menacing. "So, he had an accent like mine, and she was a *Scot*?" He took a breath. "Aristocratic Englishmen do not fall in love with Scotswomen!" It was a stereotypical comment, but he didn't care. The odds of that sort of scenario happening were slim to none, even if the Jacobite rebellion was nearly fifty years ago. "You have been duped. Don't you see?"

The two men had looked at each other and, without a word, turned to run after the man who was obviously Marcello Verdante.

Albert had followed, pilfering a boat in which to chase them across the canal to Venice proper.

Now here they were, watching the last place the fugitive may have hidden himself away. For all he knew, the information that this Verdante fellow knew the Doge of Venice may have been a fabrication. Their surveillance could easily turn into something akin to chasing a phantom. Besides, too much time had passed since he'd last seen the two, and it was likely they'd escaped anyway.

Albert sank into his musings as he sometimes did when bored.

Honestly, Gwendolyn was the most tempting bit ever to come out in London, with her amber-blonde hair and creamy skin—and those were just the beginnings of the assets. Her lips tempted a man to hold her by her ears and plunge himself into their generous depths, teeth or no. And she was rich. A good fuck and a bank account to match—there was just no comparing her to other society girls.

He just had to catch Verdante and collect that reward. Surely it would cause both Gwendolyn and Wes to see him for the hero he was. On the other hand, if this escapade didn't work out to his advantage, he probably wouldn't get another chance at making Gwendolyn his bride. It was also most likely that Wes wouldn't bring him into his inner circle, either. That being said, he was liable to have to settle for the fluffy Miss Appleton, which wasn't too bad a prospect, he supposed.

He grinned as a thought dawned on him. Ellie Appleton practically lived at the Rawleigh's house—she and Gwendolyn were nigh inseparable. That would at least get him close enough to both Gwendolyn and Wes, and eventually, they'd all be one snug little family. And if he played his hand correctly, with a pinch of luck and wagonload of charm, he could, in due course, have Gwendolyn as a playmate on the side.

His grand scheme would take some time, but would be well worth the effort in the end, though.

It's bloody cold. Albert rubbed his hands together and huffed out a breath, thinking that he could use a brandy right about now.

The more he thought about it, the more he realized that he no longer needed to be there. He'd done his job, tipped off the men as to Marcello Verdante's whereabouts. He waved one of the men over from where he was huddled next to the Campanile, the tall bell tower that had graced a corner of Piazza San Marco for centuries.

"If he emerges, come get me. In the meantime, I am going to see if I can find any more information on Verdante."

The man nodded stiffly and Albert headed for *Signore* Bernardo's palazzo.

Before reaching his room at the top of the stairs, he knocked on Wes' door to see if he had retired for the evening. When there was no answer, he crossed the hall and turned the corner to Gwendolyn and Ellie's room. He knocked, paying no heed to the fact that the sun hadn't yet risen.

Chapter Eighteen

Wes' eyes flew open, startling him from a deep, satisfying slumber and Ellie sat up next to him.

"Weston, the door," she whispered anxiously. "I must have fallen asleep."

"As did I. Ask who it is, I don't think it is Gwen. She has a key."

Ellie cleared her throat, her voice hesitant. "Who…who is there?

"Ellie, my dear, it's Albert. Is Gwendolyn with you?"

Ellie looked at Wes, shock registering on her face.

Wes felt a wave of dread crash into the center of his being. "Now why in the world would he ask that when he was supposed to wait for her?"

As Ellie made to shrug, Wes started. "Good God. Gwen!" He jumped up, threw on his breeches and scrambled to the door. Unlocking it, he then pulled it open with a force that sent a burst of wind against his body. "Albert, where is Gwen? Did you lose her? What the hell time is it?"

The only reaction Wes received from Albert was a silently inquiring eyebrow that rose above a penetrating gaze. He could only guess it was because he himself had opened the door to Ellie's room and he was half naked.

"To answer your last question," Albert said as he reached into his waistcoat pocket and flipped open his watch, "it is nearly four thirty in the morning."

"Where is Gwen, Albert?"

Albert inhaled through his nose as if he had all the time in the world, and replaced his watch into his pocket. "Don't know. I thought she might be here." He looked past Wes and into the room.

Wes cursed under his breath and pulled the door closer to his body, communicating that what went on behind it was entirely none of Albert's business.

"Sorry, dear boy. You know how she likes to hop around like the little bunny she is."

Wes clenched his jaw tight and spoke, attempting to rein in his anger. "If I recall correctly, you had offered to escort her back to the hotel when the ball was over."

"As I implied, she slipped through my hands." Albert's smile did not meet his eyes.

Wes nodded once in acknowledgment. He had to admit that if anyone was capable of doing such a thing, it was Gwendolyn. "Thank you, Albert," he muttered and made to shut him out.

Albert raised a hand and placed it on the door, preventing Wes from closing it. "If it makes you feel any more at ease, I did see her cross the canal back to Venice proper. She was in a boat," he paused for emphasis, "with a strange man."

"Thank you, Albert. That will be all." Wes forced the door closed and twisted the lock.

Albert's eyes narrowed as he stared at the exact place his *friend's* face had just been. He was not a Rawleigh servant to be dismissed so easily. It seemed that at every turn, the Rawleighs were preventing him from getting what he wanted. He'd wanted Gwendolyn for his wife, and she'd refused him. He wanted Wes for his best friend, but *Wes* had allowed others into his circle. And just when Albert had decided to try for Ellie, *Wes* took that from him as well. It was getting goddamned annoying.

They and their kind could hang for all the deprivation he had suffered at their hands.

Albert stormed down to the parlor. Some luck, however, was with him as he looked around and found himself alone. He snatched up a bottle of vermouth that had been left on one of the small tables that dotted the room. Tucking it under his arm, he then ascended the stairs once again. He'd check with the Florentines first thing tomorrow. They seemed a capricious, silly lot and most likely they would come up empty handed tonight.

* * * *

Ellie lit a candle in the room. Wes was certain she'd heard the entire conversation.

He sat down at the foot of the bed and Ellie placed herself behind him, hugging his back to her chest. "Why does Albert hate Gwennie so?"

Wes sighed. "Perhaps because his ego is still bruised from her refusal."

"It's not like Albert couldn't find someone else to wed."

Wes knew that Ellie had no idea what went through a man's head when it came to what he wanted. Hell, he could barely figure out Albert himself—and he'd known Albert for years. "You do have a point, but for now, I need to find our darling, elusive Gwendolyn." Slipping out of her arms he rose from the bed.

He quickly donned his clothes and turned to her. "I—"

Ellie shook her head, her glorious curls hanging loose about her face and shoulders as she clutched a sheet to her that only covered one of her breasts. "We don't have to talk now. Go find Gwennie and bring her back safely."

Wes smiled in appreciation before closing the door. Ellie was truly a blessing in powder and ruffles.

* * * *

Marcello could not sleep. He needed to plan their escape from the Doge's palace, and the woman who lay atop him was distracting his thoughts.

Perhaps if we fled to Sicily together, we could... No, that probably wouldn't be far enough away for his enemies to be content. And besides, he wasn't sure that Gwendolyn wished to be uprooted from her home, especially not for him.

The dilemma was familiar, and one which had plagued him ever since he became of age and the Florentine council approached him regarding his relative's fortune.

He'd grown up an only child and longed for a wife and children at his feet. He knew the day would come when he'd find the woman he wanted to settle down with. He just didn't think it would be before he reached his thirty-fifth year.

Marcello stretched to kiss the top of Gwendolyn's head as he held her tenderly in his arms. It had been so easy to tell the other women in whom he'd been somewhat interested, that it would not work beyond a few days or even a week. But Gwendolyn Rawleigh — she was the one he wanted to spend the rest of his life with, making love to her at every possible moment and to be loved in return.

With a sigh, Marcello eased his way out from under Gwendolyn. She stirred, but he soothed her back to sleep, speaking softly in his native tongue.

Retrieving a robe from the wardrobe in the bathing room, he then ventured out into the hallway to find and speak to his friend Ludovico, the Doge of Venice.

* * * *

The sky was just beginning to show the blue-grays of a brand new day, as Wes wandered about Piazza San Marco, looking for any signs of his wayward sister. In the hour or so that he'd been meandering, he'd woven in and out of alleyways and crossed bridges and back again. He'd seen nothing, heard nothing. It was as if she had never arrived on the boat from England.

Damnation.

For the first time since their father had passed away, he regretted not being stricter with his twin. Her feminine role within the gentry — the one he should have insisted she adhere to — was supposed to be a sought-after goal, not an often-snubbed suggestion. Then again, he didn't exactly allow the yoke to be slid around *his* neck, now had he? No. He'd shied away from society's rules so why shouldn't his sister follow suit? Gwen's stubbornness was entirely his fault.

He hoped to be a better Baronet than he had been a brother. The realization hit him that he should start this very moment to solidify his family's reputation. Taking a deep breath he shrugged off the guilt and sought another, more proactive, train of thought. If it hadn't been for his former lack of persistence, he would be warm in Ellie's arms, waking only to make love to her again.

Yes. His new lover was a subject worth dwelling on.

God, but Ellie was a beauty — so fine, so soft *and such a harlot behind closed doors.* He grinned to himself. She was his ideal woman. She had such a quirky sense of humor and a cute little nose, and the most perfectly responsive pearl he'd ever stroked.

Wes changed direction and made his way back across Piazza San Marco, his body aching for Ellie. He stopped short as two large men stepped into his path.

"It is too cold to be out this early without an occupation, *Signore,*" one of the men said to Wes.

"*Si*, you are quite right," he said, eyeing the Italian men warily.

"What are you doing in the Piazza before the sun has fully risen, *Signore*, if one may inquire?" the second man asked with a raised eyebrow.

"I am looking for someone," Wes replied, thinking to break off the conversation and walk away as soon as possible. He didn't trust these two. He couldn't quite put a finger on it, but something lurked just below the surface that made him uncomfortable in their presence.

"So are we," the first man said, a slow smile spreading across his face.

Wes glanced from one to the other. He'd had enough of this silly game. "I'm sorry gentlemen, I prefer a woman's company," He turned on his heel but one of the men stopped him with his words.

"No, *Signore*, you misunderstand. We are in search of Marcello Verdante."

"Well, I am not he," he muttered over his shoulder at the men and continued on toward *Signore* Bernardo's palazzo.

* * * *

Gwendolyn awakened when someone tossed open the curtains. The light was sparse, but the noise was enough to have penetrated her slumber.

"Come, Gwendolyn. I have arranged for your escape."

She sat up. Marcello was dressed in breeches and a shirt. The clothes were not his own. She could tell by the way his shoulders were stuffed into the shirt and the cuffs rode high on his forearms. "What about you?"

"Do not worry about me. Your exit from the palazzo will be a diversion for mine."

"Oh," she murmured none too enthusiastically.

"Dress yourself in that." He pointed to the edge of the bed where a dress of embroidered silk lay.

The yellow-gold of the threads stood out thickly on the cardinal background. The fabric seemed out of fashion, but she didn't express the thought aloud. "But—"

"Quickly now," he instructed, not giving her another chance to protest.

With the slightest hesitation, Gwendolyn did as he'd asked, the simple hook and eye closure at the front of the gown made for an easy toilette. In no time she was ready to leave the room and—more importantly—leave Italy permanently. The thought hit her like a sudden storm and she started to tear up at the thought. Mustering any shred of courage she could summon, she blinked the moisture into submission, determined to follow through with her plans to end her holiday and the torrid affair in which she'd entangled herself.

"Ludovico Manin is a dear friend of mine. You met him last night upon entering his palace. His guards are waiting outside the door to escort you to where he waits. You will be hidden at the bottom of his sedan chair. They will carry you into *Signore* Bernardo's parlor and from there, you will lock yourself inside your room and stay until I can come for you. It may be later today, perhaps even toward the evening, but you must stay there. It is for your own safety."

Gwendolyn nodded. Too many things ran through her head which contradicted each other. Her heart, and certainly her body, protested the fact that she was about to leave Venice behind on the very next boat she could find, had she the good fortune to gain passage for her and her party. She walked across the room and paused just before she reached for the door. This was it. This was the last time she would be in the same room with Marcello. Her hands shook.

Marcello came up from behind her and pulled her to him. "I will come for you. Do not despair."

Gwendolyn turned in his arms and lifted up on her toes, offering her lips to him.

"Gwendolyn," he whispered and took her in a crushing embrace, his mouth coming down hard on hers.

The kiss was desperate, as if he knew down deep that they would never see each other again. When he finally let her go, she couldn't face him. She wanted to remember him the way he had looked at her, looked at her body as he made love to her. She would not have been able to walk away in any sort of dignified manner if she were sloshing about in her own tears.

* * * *

From a window in the Doge's palace, Marcello had watched the sedan chair carry Gwendolyn away. Now, as he was poised at the gate they'd used to enter the palace, waiting to escape across Piazzetta San Marco, he wondered if he'd done the right thing. He could very easily have taken Gwendolyn with him, ensuring her security and at the same time, keeping his heart from being torn from his chest.

He glanced from one end of the square to the other. Finding no one about, he dashed across the Piazzetta to the covered walkway which flanked the larger Piazza San Marco. Looking over his shoulder as he past the Café Florian, he found that he had not been followed.

His thoughts once again drifted to Miss Gwendolyn Rawleigh. Perhaps he should have told her he was in love with her so she would have stayed with him without argument.

He hurried along and huffed out a sigh. Gwendolyn was intelligent, and feisty, and—as fine as sweet vermouth. Later today, he would bring her enough flowers to fill her room and confess his feelings to her. *Yes.* That's exactly what he would do. Then she would have no excuse not to wed him.

No. That would never do. If he hadn't won her heart without prancing his wealth before her eyes, if his own charms hadn't swayed her, she would never agree to enter so hastily into a life-long commitment with him.

The thought was like a heavy weight on his chest.

Crossing the four bridges then turning north toward his rented palazzo, he contemplated his situation. He was in love with a woman and was concurrently unsure of her feelings for him. It was his own damn fault. He should have told her. He should have told her while he was making love to her, while he was tasting her and feasting from her lips.

A vision of Gwendolyn's writhing body floated before his eyes. He could almost feel her, wet and ridged between his fingers. His cock began to awaken at the thought.

"*Merda*," he murmured as he entered his temporary residence and shouted for Lucio and Vas. His own voice echoed back to him, but his men didn't emerge.

That did it. After he found the two of them, he would get himself back to Gwendolyn. Things were going to start going his way, or he would run mad.

Chapter Nineteen

Much to his surprise, when Wes rounded the last corner and was passing the Bridge of Sighs, two more men, different than the ones who had conversed with him outside the Basilica, seized him by the arms and dragged him to an alcove between two shops along the walkway. Wes tensed. If it had been one man, he could've easily taken him in a fight, but as stalwart as these two looked—and the fact that he'd only gotten about two hours of sleep—he would most likely be risking his very life by engaging them both.

"Please, *Signore*, we only wish to ask you a few questions."

What is it with these Italians? "Well, you certainly fooled me. The very way you executed the brute force routine had me convinced that you were about to invite me to tea." Wes said, his voice ringing with sarcasm.

"Lucio and I are looking for Marcello Verdante. We know your sister has been in his company this evening."

Wes flinched at the confirmation. Albert said his sister had been out with a strange man. Their mother was going to kill him when she found out her daughter was ruined because her son was busy making love to his other charge. His stomach clenched. He refused to think about his mother's reaction now, not with Gwen... *Wait just a moment.* He recognized that name from somewhere. *Of course, Albert's little international game of cat and mouse.* He groaned inwardly. Those other men were in search of this Verdante as well. *Of all the men whom Gwen could have gotten mixed up with, it had to be the one all of Italy was interested in finding.*

"I am sorry, gentlemen. I have not seen my sister since last evening and never have I clapped eyes on this Verdante fellow you speak of. Now, if you would please allow me to be on my way, you shall come away from this unharmed."

To his surprise, the men released him. Without looking back, Wes headed for the palazzo.

Not two steps from the final bridge between himself and his destination, he was seized again, this time by uniformed men. He was pulled to the side as a small army escorted a sedan chair. Wes was surprised when he saw the Doge of Venice himself seated within the litter. What in the world was the Doge of Venice doing out at sunrise with an armed guard? It was the oddest thing he'd seen on holiday thus far.

Once the chair passed over the bridge, Wes expected the guards to let him be on his way, but they held him there as if he would attack their leader.

* * * *

Gwendolyn's cheeks were burning as she ascended the stairs inside *Signore* Bernardo's palazzo. She had just come from hiding underneath the robes of the Doge of Venice. Once she had alighted from his sedan in the lobby, she'd thanked him. Somehow, he had not been satisfied with mere words, so he took her and kissed her on both cheeks, murmuring something in Italian. The only words she caught were 'Marcello' and 'Verdante'. She shook herself mentally and knocked on her and Ellie's door.

"Who is there?" Came Ellie's voice from within.

"El, it's me, Gwendolyn."

After unlocking the door, Ellie threw it open. "Gwennie! Where is your key? Oh, we've been so worried!"

Gwendolyn stepped through the door, and immediately Ellie grabbed her and hugged her tightly.

She smiled drowsily and returned Ellie's embrace. "El, I just need to sleep for a little while, and —"

Ellie pulled away and held her at arm's length. "What happened to you, Gwennie? Your wig — where are your clothes?"

Gwendolyn set a hand on Ellie's forearm to convey that what she was about to tell her was serious. "I can explain."

As Gwendolyn slipped into her own nightdress, she began her sordid tale starting with the first party they had gone to on their holiday.

Ellie's eyes were wide as she listened, never interrupting her even when Gwendolyn purposefully glossed over the parts where she and Marcello had been promiscuous.

Upon the last sentence of Gwendolyn's explanation, there was a knock at the door.

"My word, you would think this was a thoroughfare," Ellie murmured before opening the door.

Just as Ellie turned the knob, the door burst open. A man, who looked an awful lot like Weston pushed Ellie into the room and shoved her against the wall. He shut the door with a kick, then proceeded to kiss Ellie frantically, raising the hem of her nightdress as he did so.

"Weston, please—"

"God, Ellie," he murmured as he kissed her.

Ellie turned away. "Wait." She sounded quite out of breath and even stranger, not alarmed in the least.

Gwendolyn stood frozen to the spot and gaping rudely at the couple, most likely.

"I can't bear to be away from you, even for a second," he moaned as he placed kisses at the corner of her mouth.

"You must—"

"Take this thing off. Let me see your beautiful body." He nipped at her lips. "Let me make love to you again."

"Wait."

"I want to lay you out on the bed and eat you in the most appalling manner."

"Weston!" Ellie finally had to shout. "We have company." She indicated with a tilt of her head to Gwendolyn, all the while trying to cover her bare legs.

He released her as if she'd suddenly caught on fire.

Ellie turned and focused on Gwendolyn, grinning woodenly. "I can explain."

Weston had the expression of a lad who had got caught with his tongue on the sugar cone.

Gwendolyn smiled to herself. She should have foreseen this affair. Ellie was her best friend, after all, and one was hard pressed to find a more wonderful man in all of Britain than Weston.

After Weston had left the room with his tail between his legs, Ellie recounted her story. Gwendolyn was sure that, just as she had done when recalling the events that happened between her and Marcello, Ellie left out many intimate details.

When Ellie finished her story, a murky silence that may as well have been a loud hum, hung in the room.

"Gwennie." Ellie swallowed. "I would be mortified if you thought ill of me because I've entered into an affair with your brother."

Gwendolyn raised her gaze to her best friend. "Ellie." She shook her head. "You must not mistake my reserved response for disappointment." She smiled, feeling rather tired but engaged. "I am more than pleased that in one fell swoop, you have avoided the horrid marriage market and have made a grand match. This is beyond my most fervent dreams for you, dearest." Ellie protested, "But there has been no understanding between me and Weston—"

"Nonsense. I will see to it personally that Weston does the right thing."

Ellie closed the short distance between them and looked Gwendolyn squarely in the eyes. "Oh, Gwennie, I don't wish to be one of those girls who attempts to force a marriage onto a man just because of her immoral behavior with him. If he loves me, as I love him, he will ask me on his own."

"But—"

"*Please,*" she begged, taking Gwendolyn by the hands and squeezing, "I couldn't live with myself if I thought for a moment that he'd been bullied into a union with me. If you love me, you will not say a single word to Weston about this."

For a moment, Gwendolyn put herself in Ellie's place. If the situation were reversed, she would not desire Marcello's family pushing him into an unwanted marriage. The single thought made her stomach lurch.

Gwendolyn nodded. "Very well. I will support you in this."

Ellie threw her arms around Gwendolyn. "Oh, thank you," she sobbed.

Enveloping Ellie in a fierce hug, Gwendolyn reassured her. "Do not worry, dear. Together we shall go back home and face our fate, whatever it may be." She released Ellie who nodded in agreement. Gwendolyn then sat down upon the bed, dreading what she was about to say next. "I-I'm afraid we must leave for home."

With no small amount of guilt nagging at Gwendolyn from the back of her mind, she observed the hesitation in Ellie's eyes. "Of course. I understand."

"Thank you, dearest."

"Does Weston know?"

"Not as of yet."

Ellie nodded. "Then I shall tell him for you. He may not react so harshly if the news comes from me."

"I think that to be a most agreeable idea, El."

With all her heart she hoped Weston wouldn't come pounding on her door asking for details of why they needed to cut their holiday short and where she'd been last night. She was optimistic that his own indiscreet evening would cause him not to press her for information.

* * * *

There was no way Gwendolyn could sleep now, not while the maid so noisily packed hers and Ellie's things. Luckily, Ellie seemed to be deep in slumber for about an hour or so.

Gwendolyn donned a dressing robe and made her way down to find someone with whom she could leave a message. She intended to ask *Signore* Bernardo to have him assist in arranging transport, *any* available transport, so that she and Ellie could get back to England as soon as possible.

Down in the parlor, she found *Signore* Bernardo, along with a few servants, rearranging the furniture. He looked up and waved her over.

"Ah, *Signorina* Rawleigh. How are you enjoying Venice?"

The elusive man of the house was a portly Italian man with a Friar Tuck hairline, albeit with more than half of his few hairs a wiry gray. "My but you are up early, *Signore*."

He chuckled. "Too much to be done for tonight's grand event! We're having hot chocolate and coffee sent over from the Florian. Will you and your party be joining us?"

"Well... May I speak to you a moment—in private?"

Signore Bernardo issued a few orders in Italian to the men in his employ then offered Gwendolyn his elbow. He led her toward the front entrance. However, she wouldn't permit him to take her any farther, lest she be seen outside by Marcello's enemies.

She turned to him. "We've had a lovely time here, and I can't thank you enough for your gracious hospitality, but I'm afraid we've run into... That is to say, we have an emergency and need to return home as soon as possible."

He frowned. "I'm so sorry, *Signorina*. Is there anything I can do to help?"

Gwendolyn felt the tension in her stomach ease somewhat. "In fact, there is. We need some sort of transport back to England. I'm afraid the ship that brought us won't be back this way for another week."

"Are you sure you can't stay? It's only a short seven days—"

"No, that wouldn't do at all. We must leave today. This very hour if possible."

Signore Bernardo thought for a moment. "There is a possibility that I might arrange passage on a cargo ship owned by my cousin. He's off to pick up a shipment of textiles of some sort from Scotland. I'm sure he'd be glad to do me this favor."

"Oh, that would be—"

"Now did he say that he was leaving today—or was that yesterday?" He said out loud to himself.

Gwendolyn's hopes plummeted.

"Let me have someone go to the docks and I can let you know if they've left or not."

"That would be exceedingly kind of you, *Signore*. *Grazie*."

He reached out his hand and patted her cheek. "*Prego, mia bella*. I will send word when I find out."

She curtsied, turned from him then headed toward the stairs, praying that the departure was in fact today and that his cousin hadn't already left.

Gwendolyn felt a bitter-sweetness in her breast as she made her way back up the stairs. She and Ellie's borrowed maid must have been finished with the packing. The girl acknowledged Gwen with a bob of her head as she passed her on the landing.

She didn't remember climbing the last of the steps, so lost in her thoughts was Gwendolyn. She would never forget Marcello, not for as long as she lived. She paused as a current of sadness flooded her being causing her to stop what she was doing. Dizzy with the feeling of not being able to breathe, she burst into her room and fell onto the bed. Hard on the heels of the next laborious breath she took, a sob burst from her throat so great she had to let it go as if she were a child. She wept loudly as her tears poured forth. The pain in her mind begged to be free of Marcello, but her heart would not permit it.

Gwendolyn nearly choked on the idea that she was in love with him. How in the world was it possible after knowing him for only two days? Marcello had accosted her several times. He had done impious things to her in a church, tossed her into the canal, embarrassed her to great excess by making her to hide beneath the robes of the Doge of Venice and put her very life in danger because he was running from something he had yet to tell her about. It was improbable if not impossible to fall in love with a man like that.

But damnation, that's exactly what she had done.

She sat up, wiping away her tears with her fingertips, thankful that Ellie had already gone to Weston with their news so that she didn't have to witness Gwendolyn's outburst. Upon reflection, she determined that she was forgetting that Marcello's situation, whatever it was, could not allow their relationship, not even on a casual level. Was he married? Had he broken the law — perhaps murdered someone? Well, it was too late now to consider the worst. Dwelling on him was a fruitless endeavor, no matter how much she wanted to fantasize that they could be together. Gwendolyn admitted to herself that her great love for him would be an unrequited one.

Why hadn't anyone ever told her that love could be painful?

Gathering her shredded emotions, she dragged herself from the bed. Gwendolyn knew she would have to leave Marcello a note telling him that she had returned home. With shaking hands, she pulled her stationery set from one of her trunks. She hoped with all her heart that he wouldn't come after her once he read the note because she knew it would be dangerous for him.

Perhaps someday…

Chapter Twenty

Wes drew Ellie into his room and shut the door. He offered her a chair near a window and stepped toward the door. *What must she be thinking?* He then turned back to her. "Ellie—"

"Weston," she interrupted, "I need to give you a message from Gwennie."

He could only blink. "Yes?"

Ellie drew in a deep breath. "Gwennie is going to cut our holiday short. She wishes to leave for London immediately."

The entire trip had been a farce, as brief as it was. The recent memories filtered through his mind, from the first moment Gwen had told him that she'd lied about having a chaperone, then when she'd found out Albert had tagged along, to the rumor that she had been fraternizing with a fugitive, up until she'd witnessed the ravaging of her best friend by her own brother. He nodded. "It is for the best, then."

"And, Weston," she began before he was able to address what had occupied his thoughts up until now. "I am of the opinion that I should return home as well.

You and I should not be abroad without proper accompaniment." He made to protest, but Ellie interjected with an additional reason. "And I'm afraid that your friend Albert would not make a very effective chaperone." She dropped her gaze to her dress and smoothed out her skirts.

Wes stood there for a moment, then held out his hand for Ellie to take. She glanced up and took his offering. He pulled her into his arms. "I think you are right. Besides, we would never see any of the sights, being in bed the whole time and all," he murmured, and nuzzled her neck.

In his arms, Ellie swayed a bit, and it made him smile.

Abruptly he lifted his head. "All three of us will leave, as soon as possible. Albert is off chasing some renegade or other. He'll never miss us."

Ellie nodded and made to pull away when he stopped her with his words. "I do, however, regret that we didn't have more time together here in Venice."

So, that was it, then. Weston didn't wish to continue with her when they arrived back to London. A fog as black as night swirled in and invaded Ellie's mind. She turned her face away then gently pulled out of his arms. "As am I," she replied quietly and headed for the door. She murmured a faint farewell to Weston.

Ellie's regret was that she had to endure looking at him, longing for him, for the forthcoming weeks on the ship bound for home. She placed her hand on the knob, and when he didn't stop her, she quit the room.

* * * *

"We've gained transport, El. *Signore* Bernardo's cousin owns a merchant ship." Gwennie held up the message she'd received not moments before Ellie had returned to the room. "It's a modern vessel. The accommodations won't be terribly luxurious, but we'll have a small cabin to ourselves, normally used for officers. They have one for Weston as well."

"Very well." Ellie couldn't have cared less if they were to be dragged behind the ship on a longboat. Current issues and painful scenarios clouded her mind, but there was no reason to vocalize the obvious. Weston hadn't declared his love, nor had he made any promises that they'd be continuing their affair once they arrived home.

So. This is heartbreak.

Gwennie stepped across the hall to alert Weston about the trip home. Moments later, he arrived to assist the valet with securing the girls' trunks while Gwennie directed them both.

While her best friend and her former lover were occupied, Ellie glanced about the chamber. She wished she could take the entire thing home with her. There were more memories for her in this room than in the whole of Venice — the bed, the blankets and pillows, the washbasin... Her hands shook a little as she tied the bow of her bonnet underneath her chin.

"We are ready, Ellie," came Gwendolyn's voice from the hallway.

Ellie took one more look around the space and sighed. Unable to even look at Weston as she passed him in the hall, she went straight for the stairs and made her way determinately through the parlor, knowing full well that Weston and Gwendolyn were right behind her. Outside, she hurried across the walkway, and stepped into the boat that would take them to the ship. She sat down, and with all her might tried not to cry, taking deep breaths to keep the tears at bay.

"I almost forgot. I need to leave this note for Albert with *Signore* Bernardo," Weston made to turn around but Gwendolyn stopped him.

"Let me, Weston. You see that the men load the rest of the trunks properly."

He nodded and handed the note to his sister. "If you aren't back in thirty seconds, I'll be forced to come after you."

She shook her head. "There won't be a need. I promise."

* * * *

On the ship, Ellie leaned on the starboard side railing staring at nothing in particular as Wes approached from the stairs that lead up from the cargo hold. The breeze blew past her only to serve as a conduit for her powdery scent that permeated Wes's very being. He inhaled, dizzy with the memory of her pale skin beneath his hands.

Gwen came up behind her. "Two more hours until we set sail. I cannot endure anymore of this torture. I swear it." she groaned.

Ellie turned to her with dull eyes. "Gwennie, why don't you go lie down and take a nap. You've hardly gotten any sleep in the last two days."

Gwendolyn nodded.

Having heard their exchange, Wes joined them. "Our trunks are secure in the hold," he said, rubbing his hands together to chase away the chill in the air.

"I think I will join you, Gwennie," Ellie said. Without even sparing a glance for Wes, she turned and headed for the companionway which led to their tiny cabins.

Gwen glared at him. "What did you say to Ellie? She hasn't been herself since we left *Signore* Bernardo's palazzo."

Wes raised his hands palms up and shrugged his shoulders.

She glowered up at him and pointed a finger inches away from his nose. "If you have broken dear, sweet Ellie's heart, Weston Rawleigh, you won't make it back to London alive," she threatened then stormed away.

What in the world has gotten into the two of them? Wes wondered as his sister crossed the deck and followed in the wake of the woman he loved. He placed his index fingers over his temples to rub away the strain. He hadn't gotten to talk to Ellie at all—hadn't been able to speak to her about their future. Hell, he was the one who should have been snippety.

How was she faring, now that they were more intimately acquainted? Did she feel the same about him as he did about her? Did she think about him every second of the day when they weren't together, just as he did? Did she even now miss the feel of him against her? Without a doubt, he certainly was aware of the cold void where her warm body should be. He felt the heat rise from his skin as he recalled her scent from a moment ago — her touch, the sound of her voice while in the throes of passion.

He sighed. Too many bloody questions were going unanswered.

His growling, hungry stomach wasn't helping matters, either. He hadn't eaten all day and wondered if the girls were similarly famished. Weston pushed himself away from the railing to see if he could fetch them some sustenance.

* * * *

Ellie flopped down onto her hard bunk as Gwendolyn entered.

"El, what's wrong?"

"Nothing," came her abrupt statement. She rolled toward the wall. It wasn't long before she spoke again but this time, her tone seemed apologetic, "Can we talk after we've had some sleep, Gwennie?"

"Agreed." With the combination of their frustrations weighing heavily on her mind, she couldn't possibly blame Ellie for her short temper. Gwendolyn climbed onto her bunk and buried her face in her hands. If they could just get out to sea and away from Italy, she could relax.

She had been unable to find *Signore* Bernardo himself so she had left Weston's note for Albert with one of the servants. She'd then glanced down at the missive in her other hand. Across the front of the envelope, written in swirling letters was a name that was as precious to her as her own—'Marcello Verdante'. She'd smoothed her fingers over it before she'd handed it off as well.

She heaved an exasperated sigh. When would Marcello find out she had gone? Likely later this evening, if any measure of good luck were on her side. Perhaps he was standing in the parlor right now, reading her note. Perhaps he was, this very instant, in a boat heading for the ship. One thing for certain, he would be madder than a hornet caught in a butterfly net that she hadn't stayed where he'd told her to.

Not an hour after Gwendolyn and Ellie had lain down for a rejuvenating nap, a knock sounded at the door. Ellie opened her eyes and turned to Gwendolyn who sat up, her eyes wide.

"Look at us, El. We are as nervous as cats."

"And we've been snapping at each other something awful," Ellie confessed. "I'm sorry."

"As am I. If anything, we should stick together."

When the second knock sounded, they both jumped.

"Gwen? Ellie? It's me, Weston. I have food."

Ellie's gaze flew to Gwendolyn's.

Gwendolyn smiled. "Come in, Wes," she called.

Weston came through the door, balancing a tray on one hand. Instantly, the scent of tea and biscuits filled the small room.

"*Signore* Bernardo's cousin is most accommodating," he said, and placed the tray of food next to Gwendolyn. "I was quite taken aback when he offered to share his rations with us. He said that they'll run out quicker, but we'll be stopping twice more along the coast of Italy before getting underway." Concluding his announcement, he settled himself next to Ellie on her bunk and looked at her.

Disregarding his nervous chit-chat, Gwendolyn observed them as their eyes met for the first time in hours, and it took Ellie a moment to cease her fidgeting and recover her wits.

Gwendolyn poured out and placed biscuits on napkins as she continued to watch Ellie and Weston out of the corner of her eye. The air crackled between them, much like the way it had between her and Marcello. Her stomach jumped at the thought of him, and her ears began ringing something awful.

She doled out the offerings and they ate in polite silence.

When the light meal was finished, Gwendolyn could no longer take the quiet. "The biscuits could have used some jam, but the tea was nice and strong. What do you think, El?"

Ellie glanced up for a scant second. She nodded and returned her gaze to Weston.

Gwendolyn cleared her throat. "Well—" She began to rise.

"Gwen, I know this is an odd request, but would you give Ellie and me a moment?" Weston asked.

"El?" Gwendolyn inquired of her friend with unspoken permission as only best friends could do.

"A moment will be fine, Gwennie." She smiled faintly.

Gwendolyn nodded. "I shan't be long." She then quit the room.

When Ellie turned her big blue eyes to him, Wes almost lost his nerve. "Er." He turned from her and went to lean on the wall for support. What the devil would he say? She was clearly vexed with him, but for what reason he knew not.

He drew in a deep breath and swung back to her before he turned chicken and abandoned the idea all together. "I-I know things have not gone as they should between us."

Ellie merely nodded. She was such a brave girl. Essentially, she could have sent his dishonorable hide from her sight, but she didn't. She sat upon the bunk, her delectable bottom lip slightly trembling, obviously waiting for him to finish his speech.

Wes growled his frustration, unable to find the words. "This whole thing is folly," he murmured and dragged a hand through the top of his hair.

"Is it?" Ellie practically whispered. "Is it folly that I love you?"

Wes's gaze flicked to hers as his breath caught in his throat. "No, Ellie," he said quietly. "It is folly that I haven't the guts to say what I need to."

She stood and took a step toward him. "Then just say what is on your mind, Weston. So much has passed between us that anything you wish to say, I shall listen to gladly. Mercy, it would be ungallant of me to deny you your opinion."

This slip of a girl who stood before him had just let him off the hook by giving her his permission to be frank. God, but he was a coward. "Then I shall just come out and say it. I love you, Ellie."

After a moment, a sweet little sound came from Ellie that was somewhere between a laugh and a sob. "Well, the hardest part is apparently over with now. Everything should be easy from here," she said tremulously, her eyes sparkling with tears.

* * * *

Walking down the companionway lost in thought, Gwendolyn heard the faint sound of murmuring voices and hurried footfalls. She approached the porthole to the deck and stopped short at the sight of Marcello Verdante struggling with at least four burly seamen.

Chapter Twenty-One

Marcello managed to throw off the assailants one by one. However, after removing themselves from the ship's deck, they reengaged him.

Following a few ineffective blows that were delivered to his face and body, Marcello managed to raise his head and bellow for the captain. Two shipmates who had been watching the fight scuttled away. In no time, the captain of the ship appeared and addressed the crowd.

"What is all this?" he rumbled, elbowing his way through the onlookers, his bushy gray eyebrows pinched together above his bulbous nose.

"Call off your men, *subito!*" Marcello growled through clenched teeth.

"Stand down," the captain commanded in Italian, indicating to the man with a lift of his bristly chin.

After the sailors had stepped away from Marcello, he straightened and dusted off his clothes, as if their hands had sullied the fabric. He then fished around in the pocket of his waistcoat.

"What is all this about? I demand to know."

"Get this ship out to sea now," he ordered, as if he were the one in charge, and tossed a handful of coins at the captain's feet. "Here is my passage."

The captain looked at him with wide eyes. "Who do you think you are to board a ship and begin demanding things of its crew, and besides, we have no more cabins —"

"You are wasting time arguing with me. Just do as I say."

"The tide —"

"To hell with the tide! I said *now*!" Marcello bellowed, then sobered just before issuing his subsequent command. "Next you are to fetch Gwendolyn Rawleigh to me," he said, tugging his shirt cuffs from the sleeves of his greatcoat as if preparing for an evening out.

From the companionway, Gwendolyn pulled back and flattened herself against the wall, her breathing shallow, a fingernail succumbing to the pinch of her front teeth. She couldn't possibly see him like this. Why he was fit to be tied! She knew him to be a passionate man, but this was downright frightening. Her heart practically pounded its way out of her corset. Good God, he would probably kill her for her disobedience, or at the very least, yell tremendously loud at her.

The captain sputtered, "The passengers are under my protection. You will have to —"

"*Gwendolyn Rawleigh!*"

Marcello roared her name so loud that Gwendolyn felt the wall behind her vibrate. She was quite sure everyone on the ship heard — including her brother.

Unable to resist Marcello's demand, Gwendolyn began her laborious journey through the portal of the gangway and across the deck to Marcello. Her legs felt heavy as she willed them to make their way toward him.

Instantly, his gaze fell upon her and his eyes narrowed. Heavens, but he was furious.

Gwendolyn swallowed and heard Weston's voice from behind.

"Who is calling for Gwendolyn Rawleigh so rudely?" his voice ground out, gaining the attention of the crowd.

"I am." Marcello glowered back.

Weston stepped around her and placed himself on the path between the mad Italian and his sister. "And who are you, to order a Rawleigh around?"

"I am Marcello Verdante, and you are in my way," he snarled and closed the distance between them in two strides.

They were nose to nose now, and Gwendolyn was pulled back by Ellie's shaking but determined hand.

"You have no business with my sister. You had better leave before this gets ugly."

"Leaving is not on my agenda today, but a beating I could fit in."

At the same time, both Weston and Marcello grabbed each other's lapels and raised their fists.

"Stop it!" Gwendolyn leaped forward, escaping Ellie's hold and shoving her arms amidst the threatening fisticuffs. "Stop it this instant!"

To her surprise, not only did the men halt the scuffle, but the captain himself was on the other side of Weston and Marcello, attempting to separate the fighters.

"That will be enough!" The captain remained ignored.

"This is none of your concern," Marcello growled at Weston. "I will speak to Gwendolyn *now*," he said through clenched teeth.

Weston pushed at Marcello with his chest. "I beg to differ. My sister *is* my concern. Are you still up for that beating?"

"Enough!" the captain shouted and shot a pistol into the air, gaining everyone's attention.

The puff of smoke was hastily blown away by the sea breeze as the captain handed the weapon back to a shipmate. "Unless you both would like to end up in the brig, you'd better cease this madness."

Weston was the first to step back. Marcello followed suit.

Gwendolyn cleared her throat. "Weston, I think I should speak with him."

Without breaking his gaze with the Italian, Weston nodded once. "I will be within arm's reach if my sister needs me," raising an eyebrow for emphasis. He then spun on his heel and headed toward Ellie.

Marcello turned to Gwendolyn. He was still glowering, his fingers flexed and extended as if they longed to be around her neck. In one swift movement, he raised his elbow for her to take.

Reluctantly, Gwendolyn placed a tentative hand over his thick arm and he escorted her to the starboard railing.

She shook, positive that Marcello would notice the shallow breaths that puffed from her lungs.

Out of the corner of her eye, she saw a few members of the crew casually making their way closer to them, as if they were set on eavesdropping upon the private conversation.

Glancing up at Marcello, she watched as his gaze snapped toward the insolent crew. He bared his teeth at them. Gwendolyn had never seen men leap away as fast as they had.

Still furious, he turned to face her, but said nothing.

Gwendolyn cleared her throat. "I know what you are going to say. You are going to ask me why I did not do as I was told."

Marcello nodded once, maddeningly slow.

Gwendolyn continued, "I fear you are not going to be appreciative of my answer."

Marcello tipped his head to the side as if to inform her she was right again.

"You have to understand, Marcello. I have done things that an unmarried lady in my social position shouldn't. I have allowed situations to happen between us that have ruined my chance to interact with good society." She fought with all her might to hold back a sob that was working hard to close her throat. "Don't you realize what I am going through? I *had* to leave Venice. I *had* to leave you, Marcello. My conscience wouldn't allow me to continue our love affair."

Marcello had closed his eyes, his emotion now hidden from Gwendolyn. Was he *that* angry with her? Why didn't he just strike her and get it over with? She wished he would at least say something to ease her trepidation. He inhaled deeply and exhaled through his nose, the sound was a frustrated one at best.

When he opened his eyes, she held her breath waiting for him to speak.

"Say it again, Gwendolyn."

She swallowed. "My conscience would not allow —"

His granite face melted into a smile. "No, *il mia nome*. Say my name," he ended in a whisper.

Gwendolyn reached out and placed a hand on the railing to steady herself. "Marcello," she breathed, while his gaze penetrated hers.

She watched his eyes close, as if the sound hurt his ears. When he opened them again, Gwendolyn could have sworn tears welled there.

Marcello reached out his arms and crushed her to him.

With a sob, Gwendolyn slid her hands up and around his neck. They held each other for several relieved heartbeats. He lifted his head and spoke, "I want you—"

Gwendolyn took a breath to revisit why she left Venice.

He placed a finger over her lips. "To be my wife."

Under his finger, Gwendolyn smiled as the realization of what he said dawned on her.

He swept the digit down to toy with her lower lip. "Where ever you are is where I wish to be," he whispered.

At that moment, a ruckus pulled Gwendolyn and Marcello's attention from each other. It was Marcello's men fighting to hold two other burley males back as they tried to get to Marcello across the deck.

"Verdante!" one of them shouted.

"W-what do they want of you?" Gwendolyn asked in a hushed tone.

"Aside from a generous helping of my fortune, they want me out of Italy." Marcello shrugged. "And I understand I greatly annoy their employer." He flashed her a smile then sobered. "Run and find your brother. Stay out of sight."

Possibly for the very first time in her life and without hesitation, Gwendolyn did as she was told.

Chapter Twenty-Two

In four strides, Marcello was across the deck bellowing to the captain, "I told you to get underway!"

Jumping at sound of Marcello's voice, he began issuing orders to get his ship out to sea.

As Lucio wrestled with one of the men, Vas had his adversary by the throat. Marcello came up and punched the man in the stomach a few times. "I told you before. Your master does not rule my life." He grabbed the man from Vas and took him to the side of the ship, which was in the process of inching away from the dock.

Marcello had no patience to wait for the ship to pull away, so he hauled the man up two sets of stairs to the poop deck. He lifted the man by the lapels of his shabby coat. "If I see you again, I will kill you," he said simply then tossed him over the railing.

He watched as the man hit the water with a splash then turned to see if Lucio needed assistance. Whether he did or not, Marcello was going to help the other Florentine off the ship as he had the first one.

On one side of the main deck, Marcello saw Gwendolyn, her friend and her brother observing the scuffle from the porthole of the companionway. Opposite them, he observed a man holding a pistol to Lucio's head, the Florentine thug still aboard ship stood behind, smiling triumphantly. The few crewmen, who weren't hauling ropes and hoisting sails, stood in a cluster off to the side, their eyes wide.

"Do not come any closer, Verdante, or I'll shoot your friend."

Gwendolyn's brother emerged from the companionway and crossed the deck. "Albert, what the devil are you doing?"

"Do not get into this with me, Weston," he sneered, "I want what is coming to me, and for once neither you nor your sister are going to interfere."

Weston narrowed his eyes at Albert. "Are you daft, man?"

"Shut up!" Albert snapped. "Verdante comes with me or his man dies."

Marcello stepped forward. "I will go, *Signore*. Put the pistol away."

"No, the pistol stays were it is. Now climb down the side of the ship, and get into the rowboat at the bottom of the chain." Albert cocked the hammer back with his thumb to show he was serious and grinned. "And by the by, Weston, upon my return to London, I fully expect your sister to accept my marriage proposal."

Everyone on deck flinched at Gwendolyn's appalled intake of breath.

Furious and clenching his teeth at Albert's last comment, Marcello stepped forward and set his foot on the first rung of the chain ladder. He paused and scanned the scene for Gwendolyn. Their gazes met from across the deck and Marcello's anger melted away. He ached for her and allowed it to show on his face. The longing in his look met the panic of hers, and without words, they said goodbye.

"Move!" Albert yelled at Marcello, and with a grin, watched the Italian's descent.

With Albert's attention elsewhere, Weston leaped for him. "Like hell Gwendolyn will accept you!" he growled, and tried to knock the pistol out of Albert's hand, but the only thing he managed to do was fling Albert's aim off target.

Taking advantage of the diversion, Lucio punched Albert in the stomach. Albert doubled over, not having been prepared for the blow. When the dry Florentine leaped for Lucio, Weston jumped onto Albert, knocking him the rest of the way to the ground. Albert held fast to the pistol, but the barrel was now pressed to the underside of his own chin by Weston's own hand.

From out of the gaping crew, Vas, who had been waiting for just the right moment, emerged to join Lucio in overtaking the Florentine, which they did with the efficiency of seasoned solders. They eradicated him from the ship, missing Marcello, who clung midway up the chain ladder, by mere inches.

In moments, Marcello vaulted back over the railing to the deck and assisted Lucio, Vas and Weston in tossing Albert over the side, but not without a few instructions.

Marcello took Albert by the back of his hair and bent his head back so that he was looking directly into his eyes. "If you so much as make your presence known to Gwendolyn ever again, I will sever your sorry manhood and feed it as *antipasto* to the pigs." Marcello hefted the slight baggage up, over and into the sea.

Everyone leaned over the railing to view the human debris in the harbor.

Ellie and Gwendolyn rushed over to stand between Weston and Marcello.

From below in the water, Albert raised his pistol and aimed it straight at Marcello. The hammer of the gun landed on its mark with a dull thud. Marcello waved insolently at Albert as they began pulling into the bay in earnest.

"That is the problem with limp, wet fuses," Marcello tossed the comment over the girls' heads to Weston.

Weston took a breath through his nose. "I wouldn't know, sir. My sharpened sword is always at the ready."

Gwendolyn and Ellie glanced at each other and giggled.

Weston turned fully to Marcello then. "So, am I to understand that you have managed to seduce and ruin my sister in the span of two days' time?"

Gwendolyn's gaze flew to Marcello's. Regardless of the lazy smile that spread across his handsome face, she turned to her brother. "This is none of your business, Weston," she warned, her fury evident.

Weston merely glanced at his sister. "I'm afraid it *is* my business, and my duty, to see that this man—"

Marcello interrupted Weston. "I have already asked your sister for her hand," he murmured then looked down at Gwendolyn, still grinning.

Weston cleared his throat. "And you didn't feel it necessary to have presented the head of her house, in this case, myself, with your suit, initially?"

"It all happened," Marcello glanced up at Weston for a moment then his gaze settled upon Gwendolyn once again, "rather suddenly."

"That is not acceptable—"

"It is so!" Gwendolyn interjected with fervor then begged, "Weston, *please*."

Smiling, Marcello reached out and drew a finger down Gwendolyn's cheek. "No, your brother has a point." He spoke softly, but loud enough for those concerned to hear. "I suppose if I had a sister, I would expect the same courtesy."

Gwendolyn felt more than saw Weston relax.

Weston nodded. "Thank you for that."

Marcello nodded a bow to Weston, an unspoken understanding settling between them.

"So, when can we expect the ceremony?" Weston dutifully inquired.

"As soon as is humanly possible," Marcello murmured, his gaze trained on his beautiful bride-to-be.

After good luck wishes were passed around, Vas and Lucio departed for shore in the rowboat that had been intended for Marcello, Albert and the Florentine thugs.

Marcello had taken Gwendolyn by the hand and bade her lead them straight to her cabin, Weston and Ellie in tow. When they arrived at the cabin, Marcello handed Weston Ellie's few personal items and shut the door, locking it from the inside.

Gwendolyn smiled to herself. It was likely that Weston led Ellie to his cabin and did the same.

She turned back to Marcello, who stood with his hands folded in front of him like a child about to be reprimanded.

"What is it?"

"I am feeling..."

"Are you ill?" She stepped toward him. There were red spots on his face from the fight that surely would turn purple from bruising. Reaching up, she placed her hand on his forehead. *No fever, thank heavens.*

"All this is wrong." He pulled away from her and indicated the cabin with a sweep of his hand. "You deserve to be properly married, in a church, then experience the delights of a honeymoon with your husband with whom you share a surname."

"Marcello—"

"I am a cad to have taken these things from you."

She understood what he was saying, and more importantly, what he wasn't. She was sure he felt that he'd robbed her of some rite of passage rituals society dictated. But he was so wrong.

"You are mistaken. You couldn't know this, but the entire reason I decided to go abroad during the season is to avoid those ridiculous traditions set forth by our foremothers and fathers. The whole notion is such nonsense to me. I despise such things. So in reality, you saved me from the humiliation of it all."

The worry etched on his brow melted away. "Are these truly your convictions?"

"I would not have said so if it were otherwise."

Marcello gathered her up in his arms. "*Mia dolce.* Never would I have thought I'd find such a beautiful, sweet, perfect mate."

Shakespeare himself couldn't have made her heart soar the way Marcello's declaration had.

She kissed him, wishing she could vanish beneath his skin and become one with him forever.

"Your lips taste so good," he murmured then reached down to gather handfuls of her skirts. "I do not think you will be needing these."

"You'll have to help me," Her own voice sounded out of breath and he hadn't even touched her yet. "I've already ruined one dress for you."

He let go of the fabric and placed his hands on her waist, effectively spinning her around so that her back was to him. He began unlacing her gown and underpinnings, and before she knew it, she stood up to her ankles in a pool of cotton and silk.

Marcello took a step back and appraised her. "My exquisite Gwendolyn."

She stood before him, unashamed of her nakedness. Unable to suppress her utter happiness, a giggle escaped from between her lips. "How I do love to hear you say my name, Marcello."

He drew her back into his embrace. "And how I love to hear you sigh mine."

The moment his mouth came down on hers and brushed back and forth, so softly that it tickled, it wasn't enough. She rose up on her tiptoes, demanding more access.

Marcello chuckled. "Patience, my love. We have the rest of our lives."

"I'm afraid I've lost all of my dignity. But it's your fault."

He grinned like the devil. "*My* fault?"

"Indeed it is."

"This may be the best thing I've ever accomplished."

"Speaking of *accomplishments*..."Gwendolyn found the closure of his breeches with her fingers and began fumbling with the fastenings.

Still smiling, he deftly maneuvered his hands between hers and in moments they stood, face to face in all their nude glory, as God intended for a man and woman so in love.

He smoothed his palms up her arms to her shoulders and back down to her wrists. "You do things to me that no woman ever has. I forever wish to be by your side."

She shivered. "Desist with the sweet words and make love to me."

Marcello took hold of her hands and sat down on the edge of the bunk. He drew her so close that she had no choice but to straddle his thighs. He leaned forward and placed a kiss on her belly.

Gwendolyn sighed. "Please. Touch me."

He placed his hands on her hips and directed her to sit. She used his shoulders to steady herself. She glanced down between them. His erection was mere inches from her opening. She tilted her pelvis, wanting far more contact when he reached down between her legs.

Her intake of breath seemed loud in the tiny space, but the whimper he elicited from her when he plunged his finger into her heat sounded like a lion's roar.

"Mmm. You *are* ready for me."

"Oh, hurry—"

Her beseeching turned to a gasp when he pulled her hips flush with his and entered her, swift and hard as steel. Once the initial shuttering ceased he guided her, rolling her pelvis forward and back, slowly, like waves lapping at the shore. He gradually increased their speed and it was all Gwendolyn could do to stay rooted to him.

A fierce storm was building inside her. The other times were nothing compared to this, he could break her very soul open, as raw and hedonistic as his actions were.

"My God, you feel so good."

His whispered words only heightened her awareness. Closing her eyes, she shook her head and moaned. "Hard—"

She didn't need to finish her plea. Marcello retracted then thrust himself deep inside her, again and again as he maneuvered her hips just as ruthlessly.

She shattered, shouting every feeling, every emotion wordlessly until she could no more. He'd come with her, his song matching hers in every way.

They held on to each other in the quiet of the cabin, worn out and slick with a sheen of sweat from their exertions.

Marcello stroked her back and she placed tiny kisses across his shoulder and neck.

"We must be out to sea by now," he commented, as the ship began rocking in earnest.

"It would be such fun to be the only two aboard, wouldn't it?"

"Just you and I, sailing around the world and back?"

Gwendolyn nodded, feeling silly that she'd voiced the fantasy aloud.

"I think I would enjoy that very much."

He hugged her to him and it that moment, she knew in her heart that he would give her the stars if she'd but ask.

* * * *

Gwendolyn was sure it would be the scandal of the century if word got back to London society about their voyage home. In fact, the entire trip would have to be accounted for. She did not look forward to that task, not at all. Why, Weston himself had admitted to everyone, on the occasion of their last supper together on board ship, that he was apprehensive about facing their mother with news of what they'd all been up to abroad. Who knew the fits her mother would throw, let alone the feminine ridicule both she and Ellie might endure?

At once her gaze took in her and Ellie's heroes, Weston and Marcello. Surely with these men on their side, the societal feminine hearts in question would not long be able to condemn them.

As they stood on the dock in Portsmouth waiting for their trunks, Weston drew Ellie back toward the gangplank.

"Weston, in case you haven't noticed, we are home now. You no longer have to travel by ship," Gwendolyn teased as she clung to Marcello's arm.

Weston smiled at his sister. "Actually, dear, Ellie and I will be continuing on to Scotland for a few days."

"Scotland! Whatever for?" Gwen asked, looking from her crazy brother to her best friend.

Weston glanced at Ellie. "Ellie has never been," he said, an irreverent grin spreading across his features.

"Ellie, is this really what you want to do?" Gwendolyn inquired, still greatly puzzled.

Ellie's glance flickered to Weston only to return to Gwendolyn. "In a word, yes." She grinned.

"But why Scotland? People only go there to do things such as hunt—or elope."

The silence that settled on the foursome drew smiles from everyone but Gwendolyn. Gwendolyn was yet staring at Ellie, waiting for an answer that would ease her confusion.

Marcello reached a hand out to Weston. "*Molti Ringraziamenti* once again for your assistance"—they shook hands—"I understand Scotland is a beautiful place for an elopement. Good luck to you."

"Thank you, Marcello." Weston nodded and smiled. "Upon our return, I have a stable of horseflesh, a cabinet of brandy and a deck of cards, all of which I am anxious to share with you, each in turn, of course."

Marcello grinned. "I look forward to being a part of your family, Weston."

Gwendolyn's eyes widened as the reason for Ellie and Weston's extended trip settled in her mind. She grabbed her best friend in a crushing embrace. "Ellie, we are going to be sisters!"

"I was wondering when you would catch on!" Ellie giggled happily.

Gwendolyn pulled away. "Do hurry back, El. I shall die of loneliness without you."

Ellie glanced over her shoulder at Marcello, then back to Gwendolyn. "Somehow, I doubt that, Gwennie."

Gwendolyn would have laughed had she not been so blissfully content with her own match. She'd never imagined she'd be so desperately in love with the man who was to become her husband.

Marcello caught her attention and she glanced up at him. His hot gaze focused on her as if she were the only woman in the world. She knew that look well. They'd better wave down a conveyance to take them to their evening's destination, post haste.

Epilogue

When Gwendolyn entered her mother's salon, the hairs on the back of her neck stood on end and a warning rang in her ears as loud as cathedral bells.

The lady of the house — dressed in her favorite rose silk gown — graced the center of her lime green velvet brocade settee like a judge at the bench, the same way she used to when Gwendolyn and her brother were about to be handed a sentence for some childish miscue.

This bodes ill, to be sure. Gwendolyn was at once pleased that she'd asked Marcello to wait just outside the door.

Judging from the look on her face, her mother had found her out.

She approached as if walking on china cups. "Hello, Mama."

Forgoing any preamble, her mother dove into the subject matter, likely as eager to get it over with as Gwendolyn was. It wouldn't affect the outcome regardless of how much mindless chit-chat they exchanged, so without question, she dismissed the possibility of pleasantries with her mother.

"Last week whilst shopping in London, I had the pleasure of crossing paths with your Aunt Arabella."

Good god. Her stomach sank to her knees. "Oh."

"We abruptly ended our shopping tour and together made our way to the Appleton's estate, determined to get to the bottom of why Arabella was still here in town and *you* were not. There, my dear, is where your plot came to light."

"I can explain—"

"You *will* explain, in writing, along with an apology for ruining Eleanor's chances—not to mention yours—of making a sound match. Not that it will be of any assistance in gaining husbands for you both. You know society will not tolerate even a hint of indiscretion! You've not only sullied our name, but the Appleton's as well."

"Mama—"

"In all the years… Of all the *imprudent* nonsense you and your brother have entertained, traveling without a chaperone is *unequivocally* the worst."

The moment her mother took a breath to continue her tirade, Gwendolyn jumped in. "Ellie and I did actually have a chaperone."

Her mother's head tilted to the side like a puppy's. "I beg your pardon?"

"I said, we did, in fact, have a chaperone."

"And *whom,* may I ask, attended you?"

Gwendolyn knew that no matter whatever silly old ninny she might name, her mother would not be appeased—even if she made one up. There would be one thing or another that she didn't approve of. And to think this whole misadventure could have been avoided had she gone ahead and invited Aunt

Arabella in the first place. Then again, she would never have been allowed the chance to be swept off her feet by Marcello. And so terribly in love that it pained her to be separated from him regardless of the fact that they'd just spent nearly three weeks at sea, sequestered together in a tiny cabin in each other's arms—naked—making love…

"Speak up, girl!"

Gwendolyn started. The volume of her mother's voice was well beyond normal. She cleared her throat. "Weston."

Her mother's face drained of all color. "I beg your pardon?"

"Weston acted as our chaperone."

"Are you saying that my Weston, your brother…laced you up…dressed your hair…saw to yours and Eleanor's things?"

"Not exactly."

"Then *what*, exactly?"

What exactly indeed. I don't suppose this would be a good time to inform her that her son is bound for Gretna Green with his other charge… Perhaps it would have been best if Weston had forestalled his and Ellie's elopement and helped her present this avalanche of devastating news to their mother. *Too late now.* "No. *Signore* Bernardo provided dressing attendants. I mean to say that Weston escorted us from place to place."

"Weston is your brother! Even if he weren't, he has not the slightest notion of how a proper chaperone conducts themselves. Has it ever occurred to you that you cannot have your head like a horse betwixt each whereabouts in which you find yourself? I've spoiled you. Your father spoiled you, and don't think for a moment that I am unaware of the copious concessions with which your twin brother continually awards you!

You must not be allowed to have your way in any and all situations in life!" She briefly pressed her palm to her forehead, then emerged to ask, "And where is your brother now?"

"I'm afraid I don't know *exactly* where he is at this moment." At least Gwendolyn could be confident in that divulgence. Besides, it was only right that Weston be on his own when he revealed to their mother *his* news. The abandonment was well deserved after leaving her in the lurch as he had. She observed her mother's gaze narrow in suspicion.

"Mama, be reasonable. Nothing hap..." Gwendolyn swallowed the end of the blatant misrepresentation. This next bit of news she knew for certain, was *not*, in fact, *nothing*. "There is more."

"More?" her mother asked wearily. "I'm not sure I'm prepared for *more*."

God help me get through this next dose. "I am to be married, Mama."

"*What?*" She came off the settee then.

"Marcello, would you please come in?"

At once, her gorgeous husband-to-be entered the salon, and her mother sank back onto the settee.

He walked straight over to her mother and held out his hand. Likely out of habitual manners, she placed her fingers into his palm.

"Mama, please allow me to present my fiancé, Marcello Verdante."

"Lady Rawleigh, it is my utmost pleasure to meet you." He bowed and brushed a kiss across her knuckles.

Gwendolyn felt a strange mix of pride and humor as she observed her mother's cheeks all sucked in and her eyes as wide as carriage wheels.

"Forgive me, my lady, but I have yet to procure a gift for my future mother-in-law."

"G-gift?" she sputtered.

"*Si*. It is tradition, is it not?"

Her mother drew in a breath, and Gwendolyn had no idea what to expect next.

"My good man, you obviously do not know my daughter and her aversion to tradition well enough to have said such a thing."

"I was thinking of *you*, Lady Rawleigh." He released her hand. "Surely you will indulge me in this?"

"Of-of course."

He turned to Gwendolyn. "Miss Rawleigh. Would you be so kind as to provide for me ink and paper?

"Certainly." She went over to the ornate mahogany and gold leaf writing desk at which she'd spent hours at as a child learning her letters and opened the main drawer. "Everything you need is within."

He strode over and sat in the matching chair. Extracting a sheet of paper, he then took up the quill and employed the ink.

Gwendolyn crossed over to stand next to her mother, who yet sat on the settee as if she was roosting.

It wasn't long before he'd folded the finished note and sealed it with the blood-red wax provided. He removed a small ring from his finger that up until now Gwendolyn hadn't noticed, and stamped the tip into the liquid. He replaced the signet and took up the missive, then blew lightly on the rapidly solidifying resin.

Marcello strode back to stand before the settee. "How long will it take a letter to get to India?" He held the note out to Gwendolyn.

She retrieved the message from him and read aloud. "It says, Raja Dhokal Singh, Pana, India."

"Do you know this individual?" Mama sounded as shocked as Gwendolyn was.

"*Si*. I have a share in his mine."

"What sort of mine?" Gwendolyn glanced at her mother, who had asked the question simultaneously.

"A diamond mine."

It occurred to Gwendolyn that she was now crushing one side of her mother's gown not moments after her knees gave out from under her, but she couldn't bring herself to rise from the settee and the pile of silk and trodden upon panier beneath her bottom.

"Forgive me, but I hope you don't mind that your gift must wait." He flashed one of his devastating smiles.

Gwendolyn slid her gaze to her mother and found that her jaw had all but unhinged.

It took a few moments, but she finally responded. "I—er... No, not at all, *son*." She grinned, more starry-eyed than Gwendolyn had ever witnessed in the older woman.

She made to stand, however Gwendolyn yet pinned her down. "Get up, then."

"Oh, pardon me, Mama." She stood and Marcello immediately came to her side.

"I must attend to my private correspondence now. Please do make yourself at home, M-Marcello." She said his name as if trying out a foreign word for the first time which, Gwendolyn supposed, was actually the case.

After her mother swept from the room, Gwendolyn turned into the already waiting embrace of her betrothed.

"I've never seen anyone move a woman like you can. I'll have to keep my wits about me from this day forward."

His face flushed and he shrugged a shoulder. "I will confess that you were more difficult to read when first we met."

Now it was Gwendolyn's turn to blush as she remembered how she'd conducted herself that night at the ball in Venice. "My behavior was—"

"Provocative," He drew her in close and his lips brushed her temple. "Rousing," he kissed her nose. "Irresistible." His mouth claimed hers softly, as if in utter reverence and the room seemed to spin.

She pulled away enough to speak. "You realize that fornicating under my mother's roof—no matter what size diamonds you offer her—is strictly forbidden."

"I will appear the ever-dutiful son."

"Good."

He hugged her tightly again. "Did I tell you I'm as good at sneaking around as I am at reading women?"

She stomped her foot, managing to avoid his toes. "Marcello Anthony Verdante!"

He chuckled. "Do not worry, I shall do it for your mother."

That's it. He's gone mad. "How do you figure?"

"Well, she *did* say that you must not be allowed to have your way in any and all situations in life."

About the Author

Born and reared in Southern California, Genella DeGrey longed to be your typical blonde, tanned, surfer girl but failed miserably. Unable to sit idle without falling asleep, she embarked upon several artistic endeavours. Make-up and set dressing for the entertainment industry, Resort Enhancement for The Walt Disney Company and writing sexy historical romance top the list of her favourite activities. A consummate closet goth and amateur music and (red) wine enthusiast, she is also a hopeless romantic awaiting the arrival of her very own Mr Romance/Soul Mate with whom to share the rest of her life.

Come and visit her on the web at genelladegrey.com

Genella DeGrey loves to hear from readers. You can find her contact information, website details and author profile page at http://www.totallybound.com.

Totally Bound Publishing